The Nude on the Postcard

The Nude on the Postcard

Regis McCafferty

Creators Publishing
Hermosa Beach, CA

The Nude on the Postcard
Copyright © 2018 Regis McCafferty

Cover art by Peter Kaminski

CREATORS PUBLISHING
737 3rd St
Hermosa Beach, CA 90254
310-337-7003

ISBN (print): 978-1-945630-89-7
ISBN (ebook): 978-1-945630-88-0

First Edition
Printed in the United States of America
1   3   5   7   9   10   8   6   4   2

Contents

Regis McCafferty

INTRODUCTION

Introductions are not common to fiction, particularly an introduction to a mystery where the protagonist is a private investigator in New York City more than a year prior to America's entry into World War II. Europe was at war, but the United States was still months away from the attack on Pearl Harbor.

In March 1936, the German American Bund was established and elected a German-born American citizen, Fritz Julius Kuhn, as its leader. Kuhn was a veteran of the German Army in World War I and a member of the Nazi Party who had been granted American citizenship in 1934. The high point of the Bund's activities was the rally at Madison Square Garden in New York City on February 20, 1939, when some 20,000 people attended and heard Kuhn criticize President Roosevelt by referring to him as "Frank D. Rosenfeld" and calling his New Deal the "Jew Deal." But the point to be noted is there was substantial German and pro-Nazi sentiment in some New York City communities, most notably Yorkville, commonly known as Germantown, on the Upper East Side. In fact, during the 1930s, Yorkville was the New York City base of the German American Bund, the notorious pro-Nazi group.

Even before U.S. involvement in World War II, Nazi strategists, including the Abwehr, the German intelligence agency, began inserting operatives into American cities or turning German-American citizens to the Nazi cause. One example would be Maximilian Gerhard Waldemar Othmer, German born, who came to the U.S. in 1919. He became a naturalized citizen, married an American woman, and settled down with his family. In spite of the fact that he made frequent trips to Germany, no one guessed that Othmer was a sleeper agent for the Abwehr. He became involved with the pro-Nazi German-American Bund, eventually becoming the leader of the Trenton, New Jersey, branch while working in the Brooklyn Navy Yard. After establishing himself as a hardworking, average guy, he got a job at the Camp Pendleton military base in Virginia, on the orders of German intelligence. In this position, he was able to send information to his handlers in Germany about British and American military vessels, convoys, and merchant ships in the port as well as Allied ship movements.

When war broke out in Europe in September 1939, President Franklin Roosevelt declared that while the United States would remain neutral in law, he could "not ask that every American remain neutral in thought as well." Roosevelt himself made significant efforts to help nations engaged in the struggle against Nazi Germany and wanted to extend assistance to those countries that lacked the supplies necessary to fight against the Germans. Military goods, food, and raw materials flowed from the United States whether publicly acknowledged or not. There was much information to be gained in and around the ports of New York City, information useful to the Nazis, and what better place to pick up information than bars and brothels.

This story, *The Nude On The Postcard*, is about the search for a young woman who has been turned into a drug addict and put to work in a brothel in order to provide money and information for the Nazi cause in America. This novel is fiction, not based on actual events, but written in the supposition that those events could, and probably did, take place.

As a work of fiction, references to real people, events, or locales are intended only to provide a sense of authenticity and are used fictitiously. Other characters, incidents, and dialogue are drawn from the author's imagination.

WWII TIMELINE

FROM MARCH 1938 TO APRIL 1940

March 11–13, 1938: Adolf Hitler, Führer of Germany, is cheered in the Reichstag after announcing the union with Austria. Immediately after the union, Nazis began a brutal crackdown on Austrian Jews, arresting them and publicly humiliating them.

September 29, 1938: Germany, Italy, Great Britain, and France sign the Munich agreement, which forces the Czechoslovak Republic to cede the Sudetenland, including the key Czechoslovak military defense positions, to Nazi Germany.

March 14–15, 1939: Under German pressure, the Slovaks declare their independence and form a Slovak Republic. The Germans occupy the rump Czech lands in violation of the Munich agreement, forming a Protectorate of Bohemia and Moravia.

March 31, 1939: France and Great Britain guarantee the integrity of the borders of the Polish state.

April 7–15, 1939: Fascist Italy, ally of Germany, invades and annexes Albania.

August 23, 1939: Nazi Germany and the Soviet Union sign a nonaggression pact and a secret agreement dividing eastern Europe into spheres of influence.

September 1, 1939: Germany invades Poland, beginning WWII in Europe. France and England honor their agreement to defend Poland and declare war on Germany on September 3, 1939.

September 17, 1939: The Soviet Union invades Poland from the east.

September 27–29, 1939: Warsaw Poland surrenders September 27. The Polish government flees into exile and Germany and the Soviet Union divide Poland.

November 30, 1939–March 12, 1940: The Soviet Union invades Finland, but has a difficult time of it. Finland eventually sues for an armistice that cedes the northern shores of Lake Lagoda and the small Finnish coastline on the Arctic Sea to the Soviet Union.

April 9, 1940–June 9, 1940: Germany invades Denmark and Norway. Denmark surrenders immediately. Norway surrenders June 9.

PROLOGUE

He opened the door, stepped inside, paused, then closed it behind him. The room was small, but big enough for the business conducted in it. She was sleeping on a double bed, or at least appeared to be. Hard to tell, he thought, considering the drugged state she was in.

He walked quietly to the bed, reached down, and lifted the thin satin sheet that covered her. She was naked underneath the sheet, as she should be. Slender, firm breasts, curly chestnut hair between her legs, the same shade as the long wavy hair that fell to her shoulders. Without opening her eyes, she raised her arms as if to embrace someone, anyone. "Good time," she said, softly, "Good time ... make love."

"Well, yes, you are that, sweetie," he whispered, "a good time," though he doubted she heard. She had been a good time before and after he introduced her to cocaine and heroin. And weed, of course. Marijuana was a good beginning and easy to get. Same with cocaine. Heroin was a bit more difficult to come by and more expensive, but it made the women pliant.

Coke to take them up and horse to bring them down, but not so far down they couldn't screw five or six dockworkers day or night. Food, some personal items, a few bottles of booze, and occasional change of bedding were his only expenses aside from dope. There was Bertha, of course, the woman who ran the house for him, but she only cost him seventy-five a week. He suspected she skimmed a bit off the week's receipts, but it was negligible, and he doubted he could get another live-in as cheap.

With ten to twelve girls in his stable, it usually netted him eight hundred or more per week after expenses, a tidy sum considering the average Joe was knocking down twenty-five bucks for six days' work—if they were working. 1940 was better than the past few years, but times were still damned tough. But just like booze, guys always seemed to scrape together enough money for sex. Of course, half of what he took in went to the cause, but that still left plenty for an upscale apartment, nice car, clothes, money in the bank, and some high living.

Another benefit to his operation was the information the women were able to gather from dockworkers and an increasing number of soldiers from the Army Terminal, information on cargo bound for Europe. His girls picked up sailing times, cargo, and an occasional bill of lading that included destination—information he could pass on.

He was Nazi through and through, and the *cause*, as he called it, wasn't something public like the German Bund. No, the cause was more important: secret, clandestine, and the source of critical information funneled to the Fatherland, the Reich. In any case, the Bund, which had ridden so high with the rally at Madison Square Garden early in 1939, had collapsed with the arrest of its leader, Fritz Kuhn, for embezzlement in December of '39.

There were nine women in his house now—twelve, a couple weeks ago. He had to terminate three of them. The cops found the body of one in the Hudson. The other two bodies had never shown up. Probably washed out to sea. Just as well, he thought. They'll be missing persons for eternity with family always hoping … He smiled, not knowing why he took pleasure in that thought, but he did. And this one on the bed, this little Annette, might be next if he didn't get a bit more action out of her. If so, he'd have to find four replacements instead of the three he hoped to add over the next couple weeks.

Regis McCafferty

ONE

I slipped my right hand inside my coat and wrapped it around the butt of my .38 snubnose. Twenty feet from the entrance to my building I paused, staring through a couple double-double bourbons and nighttime fog. There was someone hunched over in the alcove—someone wearing a dark raincoat. Not moving, not snoring, just crouched like a cat ready to spring. In my neighborhood, it could be a drunk, but if it was, it was the first in my memory to sleep it off in the doorway of my building.

I eased the .38 out, held it to my side, and walked slowly to the edge of the alcove. Whoever it was never moved.

I stepped away from the edge of the building to in front of the alcove. "Hey, bud! Better get a move on before some cop comes along and runs you in."

The head, covered by a battered gray fedora, came up and two large brown eyes looked at me. With a slight movement, the raincoat fell open and two thinly veiled breasts stared at me. It was a woman, for Christ's sake!

She started to rise slowly, using the alcove wall for support. About two-thirds of the way to a complete standing position, she stopped, tilted her head back, and looked directly at me. "The door is locked."

I debated. Not whether to answer but whether to put my snubnose away. She looked harmless enough. I put it back in the holster. "Yeah, it's locked. Why do you want in?"

"I gotta pee."

I didn't say anything.

She hesitated, then, "See someone."

"Who?"

"Detective. Max Grant."

"Why do you want to see Mr. Grant?"

"I gotta pee." Another pause. "Business."

I couldn't tell if she was drunk, slow, or maybe just cold. It was near the end of March 1940, and it had been raining, a cold rain, and spring hadn't sprung.

"It's almost midnight, lady. I think you missed business hours by a few."

She was now shivering. "Im—Im—Important."

I'm always telling Pepper, my office manager and associate, how curiosity can get you in trouble, and I speak from experience. But what the hell: she had to pee, right? I took the key from my pocket, opened the door, helped her stand upright, and guided her in. She just stood, unmoving, as if in a trance.

I closed the door, heard the lock click in place, and took her arm. "The office is three flights up. Can you make it?"

"Yeah … Gotta pee.

I was hoping that once she relieved her bladder, it would relieve her mind, and I'd find out what was so important.

My office on Flatbush, in Brooklyn, is also my apartment. It's a corner set of rooms on the third floor of a four-story building that consists of an anteroom, office, bed-sitting room off the office, and a bathroom that can be entered from the anteroom or bed-sitting room. I kept the bathroom door to the bed-sitting room locked, for obvious reasons. It's convenient. It's also cheap, or at least cheaper than maintaining an office and separate apartment. And it's only a ten-step walk to work. I'd been a tenant long enough that the owner trusted me with a key to the front door—that, and the fact he quickly got tired of me phoning late at night to get in.

We entered the anteroom to my office, and I guided her to the bathroom with a word of advice: "Flush."

"Of course."

Hell's bells, I thought, two new words. We're making progress. While my guest was relieving herself, I went into my office to the small cabinet set into the bookcase on the wall across from my desk—my stash cabinet. The only things stashed are glasses, booze, and tobacco. I took out two glasses, a bottle of bourbon, set them on my desk, and plopped my butt in one of the side chairs.

Two minutes later, I heard the toilet flush and the water come on in the basin. She came out of the bathroom a minute later, paused to look around Pepper's domain, then walked into my office to take a seat in the other side chair. She had her coat over her arm but was still wearing the hat. I wondered if she slept in it.

Nope. She took it off and set it on the floor along with a small, leather shoulder bag. She wasn't bad looking for a dame who I guessed was in her early to mid-forties, though tonight, she looked like she'd been rode hard and put away wet. Slender, good figure, about five-two with brown hair and eyes, and no wedding ring. She was eyeing the bourbon. I poured a tot for both of us.

She tossed it off, set the glass on the desk, and pushed it toward the bottle. I poured another for her.

This one, she sipped. "You Max Grant?"

I nodded. "That's me."

Max Grant, private investigator in New York City at the end of a cold and windy March of 1940. Thirty-five years old, just shy of six feet, dark brown hair and brown eyes, heavy mustache, and 175 pounds if I've had a good meal that day. Ex-cop, ex–credit chase man, ex–car owner, ex-steelworker, ex-married, ex-ex. Ex–cigarette smoker as well. I gave them up a few months ago and switched to a pipe. Went from three packs a day to just a few butts in a week. Depends on how much of a hurry I'm in. It's also made a difference in climbing three flights of stairs to my corner office.

"Got a cigarette?"

I stood, walked to my stash cabinet, took out an open pack of Luckys and placed it on the desk in front of her. She took one and put it in her mouth.

"Match?"

I fished a box of matches out of my pocket and set them on the desk while thinking, all she needs now is a kick in the lung to get her started.

I pulled my pipe and tobacco pouch from my pocket, saw the pipe was still half full of tobacco, so lit up.

"All right, miss, you peed, had a drink, are now enjoying a cigarette, and it's almost midnight. What's so urgent that it couldn't wait till tomorrow?"

She took a pull on the cigarette. "My daughter is missing. Jake said you could find her." She had a dry, whiskey voice, a voice that reminded me of Marlene Dietrich.

"Jake?"

"Jake comes to the Bowery Mission a couple times a week for a cot and a feed. He said you find people. Said he helped you find a woman named Bennett."

She was right. A fellow from the Mission named Jake did help me find a woman named Sarah Bennett back in December of the previous year. Miss Bennett was a courier—she carried information between scientists in Europe and the US—who had been kidnapped by Nazi agents. Jake also had a talent for picking locks.

"Yeah, I remember Jake. Good man. But let's start at the beginning. What's your name?"

"Emmanuelle Fouchet, but everyone calls me Elle."

"Very French, but you have no accent."

"I was born here. My parents emigrated from La Rochelle. It was only when I was eighteen that I went to France."

"Where do you live?"

"Here and there. Rooms sometimes. Women's shelters, mostly."

"No job?"

"Not what you'd call regular."

I didn't pursue it. We both knew how she could earn money on the streets. "I take it your daughter doesn't live with you."

"She was born in France and lived with me there till she was fifteen. We came back to the states in '33 for a year. I returned to France but she wanted to stay in America. She lives with my sister in Sunset Park."

"When did she disappear?"

"Almost two weeks ago."

I reached for a pad and pencil on my desk, checked my calendar and wrote down the date. "What's her name?"

"Annette Fouchet."

"Fouchet your married name?"

"No. Never married."

"How old is Annette?"

"Twenty-two."

"Father?"

She just looked at me with what some would call a blank expression.

"We'll skip that." I took a moment to relight my pipe.

She took a deep drag on the cigarette. She was braless, and the salient points under her sheer blouse rose and fell as she inhaled and exhaled. I had no doubt she could still make it on the streets, at least for the next couple years, though my guess of early forties was correct. Damned well preserved, considering the life she must have led, but some women are like that. They're lucky enough, or have the right family ancestry, to retain their looks and figures into their fifties.

"Okay, Elle, here's the way it is: We don't work for free. Our fee is forty-five dollars per day plus expenses, with less than a day prorated. We require a one-hundred-dollar retainer, but that's applied toward the fee. If we should find her in a day, you'd receive a refund of fifty-five dollars less expenses. To be honest, you don't look like you have that kind of money."

"I have something else."

Of course, the first thought that came to my jaded mind was sex for service. It had been offered on occasion in the past and declined. Don't get me wrong, I'm not a Goody Two-shoes, but I have no desire to become a regular at the local clinic. In addition, I have a serious relationship going with a fine lady that would come to a screeching halt if I shared a dose of what the newspapers call a social disease.

She surprised me. She lifted her bag from the floor, pulled out a small leather pouch, loosened the drawstrings, and out trickled into her hand what appeared to be three rubies. They were blood red, cut and at least five carats apiece, maybe more. She placed one of them on my desk.

"Have it appraised. It should be worth a week or ten days."

My first thought was, the rocks are hot. I mean, think about it. This woman is obviously down and out, living part time on the streets, getting meals at a mission or a soup kitchen, and certainly not a fashion statement in clothes. But she sits here and calmly dumps what is probably a thousand bucks worth of stones into her hand. My expression must have shown what I was thinking.

She nudged the glass again for another bourbon.

"They're not stolen."

I poured. "Can you prove it?"

"Yes, but not tonight. I have the letter that came with them, but not with me." She paused. Then went on. "I lived in Paris for most of the past twenty-five years, returning to the states only three times. I was almost nineteen when I first arrived in France and immediately found work as a model." She paused again and picked up her bag. She shifted a few things around and produced an envelope that she handed to me. "That's a photo of me taken in 1914. It's important because my daughter looks exactly as I did back then, so much so that except for twenty-five years' difference, we could be mistaken for sisters."

I lifted a postcard from the envelope. It was Elle, no doubt, and partially nude. The card was from a Paris salon and obviously from some years ago. She was still attractive today, but was certainly quite beautiful then.

She took a sip of her drink. "It's a long story, but the rubies were a gift and gave me a way out of France: The Germans are on the move and have France in their sights. I originally had seven rubies. Those three are what I have left."

I put the postcard back in the envelope and handed it to her. "It's late. Where will you stay tonight?"

"I don't know. Somewhere."

"I want my associate to hear all this, and more, tomorrow. You can sleep on the couch in the other office. You can use the bathroom for the next half hour. After that, you'll have to hold it till about seven in the morning because I'll lock the door. That okay with you?"

She actually smiled. "Yes. That's kind of you."

I put the booze away, got her a pillow from my double bed, and a spare blanket, before shutting the door to my office and going to my bed-sitting room.

Forty minutes later, as I was drifting off, I mumbled, "A few months ago it was the nude on the cigarette case, and now it's the nude on the postcard. What next?"

TWO

Next was morning. Early. Elle was still sleeping after I finished my morning bathroom routine, so I unlocked the bathroom door to the anteroom, and locked the door that led from the bath into my bed-sitting room.

My morning routine had changed. What used to be a cigarette before, during, and after coffee had been replaced by the ritual of selecting a pipe and filling it with one of several tobaccos I kept on hand in my cabinet. This morning, I chose a pipe I'd bought the week before, a smooth bent Peterson pipe that Jake Resnick suggested I buy when we visited a midtown tobacconist.

Jake was an old friend, an emigrant from Russia in 1921, and inveterate pipe smoker for more than 40 years. His name when he landed here was Jacob Ben Reznikov, but when he opened a small photographic studio on Livonia, he changed his name from Reznikov to Resnick. He said he thought Resnick was more American and would improve his business. I don't know if it did, but he was still in business at the same location and had picked up a sideline of dealing in antiquities.

Now, at 60 years old, with gray, unkempt hair and mustache, hazel eyes, and a slight stoop, Jake had enough wrinkles in his face to put a prune to shame. But his hazel eyes always held a twinkle and he had a wry sense of humor and wit that was quick and spontaneous. And he was a pipe smoker who always had a pipe in his mouth, lit or unlit. It was Jake who first helped me pick out a couple pipes from a local tobacconist's shop when I decided to try to kick the cigarette habit.

I put a pot of coffee on, filled my pipe with a Virginia and Burley blend that Jake had also suggested, took a few puffs, and then set it in the ashtray. Pepper and I usually have coffee and Danish delivered by the local deli, but I figured Elle could probably use a cup of java when she woke. She must have been dog tired, because she was still sleeping, blanket almost to the top of her head, and curled in a fetal position facing the back of the couch, when Pepper came in.

Pepper is Negro, or colored, or black—I'm never sure of the proper terminology, not that it makes a damn bit of difference to me—but her name is actually Paula Brown. She and another young girl of the same age, also named Paula, but white, were raised in a foster home. The foster mother, who was Negro, nicknamed them Salt and Pepper to remove confusion if she called for Paula. Pepper's tall, slender, very attractive, in her late twenties, and she wears a light gardenia perfume, which is the primary reason I hired her. I'm a pushover for gardenia. The fact that she had a couple years at City College, is extremely efficient, and knows more about running an office than I ever will didn't enter into the decision. Or at least that's what I tell myself.

Pepper dropped her purse on her desk and turned to hang her coat on the coat tree when she spotted

Elle. I was standing in my office just inside the door as she turned toward me and raised an eyebrow.

I moved into the doorway. "She had to pee."

"Huh?"

"For real. Turns out she was a midnight client. She was waiting last night, crouched in the alcove, and the first words she spoke, after 'The door is locked,' were 'I gotta pee.'"

"Did she?"

"Did she what?"

"Pee."

"Yep."

"That's a relief. I was having nasty thoughts of what it would cost us to have the couch re-covered."

The deli delivery arrived at the same time the blanket on the couch stirred, turned over, and looked directly at me. "I gotta pee."

The deli delivery guy stopped dead, looked at Elle, then me and Pepper, shrugged, set the coffee and Danish on Pepper's desk and walked out.

I looked at Pepper. "Sounds familiar." Then, to Elle: "The bathroom door is open and I made a fresh pot of coffee. How do you take it?"

"Just coffee." That was said over her shoulder as she hustled through the door.

Pepper took her coffee and Danish out of the sack, then handed the sack to me. "What's the story?"

"I'll let her tell it when she comes out of the bathroom. The weather was foggy last night and so was I, so I could stand to hear it again. This much I know: her daughter is missing, and she wants to pay for our services in rubies."

"Rubies? You're shitting me."

"Nope. I saw them."

Elle came out of the bathroom as I poured her a cup of coffee. After I made introductions, I said, "Come into my office. I want you to tell Pepper what you told me last night but in more detail. You want a Danish with your coffee?"

"No, but a tot of bourbon in the cup would be nice."

Pepper's eyebrow went up again, but she didn't say anything. I got the bourbon out of my cabinet and poured about a shot into Elle's coffee.

"Okay, Elle, let's start at the beginning: you say your daughter is missing, and you told me she's been gone for a while. Tell us about it."

"I came back to the States the first week in November, about five months ago, and toward the end of the month, we began meeting at a small deli every Tuesday evening after she got off work. We'd have coffee or Coke and just talk. Catch up, really. I'd been living in France for almost seven years. I came back once in that time and then only for a month."

"Why didn't you meet at your sister's place?"

"We don't get along well. She doesn't approve of me. Aside from that, if it was just the two of us we could talk freely without another set of ears listening in. Anyway ... a week ago last Tuesday, she didn't come to the deli. I didn't worry much; that had happened once before. She'd had to work late doing translations."

I took a sip of coffee. "Where does she work?"

"Until January, Saks Fifth Avenue, in women's shoes, but she had applied for a position as French translator for some scientists at the physics lab at Columbia University. When it was offered, she took it."

I looked at Pepper, who was smiling. The woman I was dating, Ariella Blumfeld, was a manager at Saks, and we knew a little something about physics labs. "Okay, go on."

"When she didn't show the following Tuesday, I got worried. Bit the bullet and visited my sister the following day. That's when I found out she'd been gone for more than a week.

Pepper spoke up. "Boyfriends? Steady?"

"She dated a guy while she was at Saks. He worked there. I think she continued to see him after she took the job at Columbia, but she hasn't mentioned him lately."

"Name?"

"David ... last name started with a 'B.' Spelled it funny ... Oh, it's Braun. Like in Brown but spelled different."

"Still work at Saks?"

Elle gave Pepper a look that said, "How the hell should I know?" but simply replied, "No idea."

I lifted my pipe from the ashtray and lit it. "Okay, Elle. We'll need one of your rubies to have it appraised, and we'll need your sister's name and address. We also need to know where to contact you."

"I'll get a room somehow, and let you know where."

I looked at Pepper. "Get her twenty-five bucks out of petty cash. We'll add it to the fee." I turned to Elle. "Get a place that has a hall phone. Pepper will give you one of our cards. Call us and give us phone number and address. I want to be able to get hold of you if we have questions. And Elle?"

"Yeah?"

"That twenty-five should cover everything for a week or more, so I'll be blunt. Stay off the streets at night. I don't want to have to come looking for you if I need you."

She stared at me for a few seconds. "You may have me figured wrong."

"Maybe—but it really doesn't matter, does it? If the ruby's worth what you say it is, you've hired us. But it's a two-way street. You're part of this, too."

"The ruby's good."

I thought she was going to ask for another hit of bourbon, but she didn't. She stood, walked into the anteroom while talking with Pepper, slipped on her coat and hat, and left without another word. I took a sip of coffee. Cold. So was my pipe. I suspected the day would match both.

THREE

I laid my pipe in the ashtray, walked into Pepper's domain, and filled my coffee cup. "Well, whatcha think?

"I think we don't have much to go on."

"Yeah ... but we've been there before. Did you get her sister's name?"

"Anna Helgesen."

"Sounds Norwegian. Address?"

"Manhattan. Hell's Kitchen from her directions. She didn't know the number, so I'll give it to you the way I got it. Go up Ninth Avenue. I assume she means go north. At Forty-fourth Street, turn left and it's the second brownstone on the right. She said her sister owns it and it has three apartments. The sister lives on the ground floor and rents the other two out."

I took a sip of coffee. "Sister's husband?"

"Widow. I didn't get details. Maybe she doesn't know. She did give me the ruby. I have it in an envelope."

"When you get down to it, she doesn't know squat. But that's what she hired us for—or *maybe* hired us for. Depends on the ruby. I'm going to visit the sister. Transfer the phone to the answering service and take the ruby to Rose's jewelers in the next block. Get a written appraisal."

"Will do. How's Ariella?"

"Ornery."

Pepper smiled. "Oh? Pickin' on you again?"

"You could say that. I had dinner at her place last evening and was all set to play mattress games when she said I'd have to go back to my own cave for the night. Seems they're doing a quarterly inventory at Saks and she wanted to be there before seven in the morning. Said if I stayed, she'd be lucky to get there by nine."

"Undoubtedly true. And you wouldn't have shown up here till ten, missing the lady who had to pee. You probably would have stood in the front doorway, scratching your head, trying to figure out where the puddle came from."

"My, you're quick this morning."

"That's what Bo said 'bout an hour and a half ago."

"Jesus! I gotta get out of here! I'll visit the sister while you get an appraisal."

Alexander Bowe, known as Bo to one and all, is Pepper's live-in boyfriend, and at a strapping six-three and 220 pounds, he's big enough to fill the doorway when he occasionally comes to pick up Pepper. I shook hands at arm's length the first time I met him, but he's a gentle lad who adores Pepper and treats her like royalty.

I thought about packing my .38 snubnose but instead just slipped on my coat and tweed newsboy cap, put my pipe and pouch of tobacco in my pocket, headed out the door, and then down the stairs. At the front door I paused, debating whether to take a cab or bus. Decided on the bus till we found out if the ruby was kosher. I took my pipe from my pocket, tamped and lit it, then walked to the bus stop at the end of the block. I'd been waiting for about ten minutes and had just knocked the ash from my pipe when a bus came along that would take me to lower Manhattan. I'd have to transfer to another that would take me up Eighth Avenue but that was all right. The weather was decent, just shy of fifty degrees and clear. I enjoy riding the bus, or trolley, or even a taxi. Truth be told, I'm a people watcher when I have the opportunity, and enjoy having my butt carted around while I immerse myself in the melting pot that is New York. I've traveled a bit, was a cop for a few years, worked construction in the Midwest, bummed around for a while, but I always seem to somehow find my way back to the big city.

I managed to get a window seat two-thirds of the way to the back of the bus, and staring out the window, watched the city slide by. As we crossed Brooklyn Bridge, a liner was passing underneath, headed out to sea. Had it been a freighter, it could have been going anywhere, but it was a luxury liner with three white stacks, and chances are, it was headed for Europe. Maybe England, or France, or Italy ... who knows? But I daydreamed myself on board, in the company of Ariella, sailing for France. We'd been dating—a socially acceptable term for sleeping together—for three months, and though marriage hadn't been discussed, it was something I knew both of us thought about. Maybe someday.

I transferred to another bus, and after jogging west on Canal Street, it turned north on Eighth Avenue. It gave me an extra block to walk, but the weather was decent. The last time I'd been anywhere near Hell's Kitchen was when we managed to rescue Sarah Bennett from some Nazi wannabes. Sarah was a courier of information between scientists in the States and Europe, and was carrying information the Germans wanted. They didn't get it.

I dredged up some old memories of Hell's Kitchen, also known as Midtown West. It's located between

Thirty-fourth Street on the south, Fifty-ninth Street on the north, Eighth Avenue on the east, and the dock area of the Hudson River on the west. Actually, those borders are a bit vague and fuzzy, as is the history of how Hell's Kitchen got its name. The one story that seems to have traction, or at least is more often repeated, is a tale from back in the late 1800s. A veteran police officer by the name of Dutch Fred was patrolling an area of West Thirty-ninth Street with a rookie cop when they came onto a small riot. The rookie commented that this place was hell itself. Dutch Fred replied, "Hell is a mild climate: this place is Hell's Kitchen." No one knows for sure if that tale is true, but the name is memorable, and a hundred years from now, it'll probably be called the same.

One thing that is certain is that for more than 80 years, gangs fought over and ruled Hell's Kitchen. With gangs such as The Hell's Kitchen Gang, the Gorillas, the Parlor Mob, the Westies, and the Gophers, the neighborhood became known for its violence. In Gopher territory, a gang known for lurking in cellar stairwells, it was said no other gang stepped foot in their turf without permission. The violence escalated during the 1920s after Prohibition became law in 1919. The many warehouses in the district served as ideal breweries for bootleggers who controlled the illegal booze. Gradually, earlier gangs, such as the Hell's Kitchen Gang, were transformed into organized-crime entities, about the same time Owney Madden became one of the most powerful mobsters in New York. It wasn't as bad now, but still not an area to take a nighttime stroll with your sweetie after ten o'clock.

I got off at Eighth and Forty-second, walked west, crossed Ninth Avenue, and stopped in front of the second brownstone a minute for a look-see before climbing the dozen or so stone steps to the front door. Empty flower boxes graced the ledges beneath the two front windows, and there was a large clay pot to the left of the door but no flowers in it. Several feet away, a forlorn tree, about eight feet high, grew in an empty space at the edge of the sidewalk. Maybe a maple, maybe not. It looked dead, but hell, it was early days yet.

The buzzer panel had three buttons: "Owner," "Barstow," and "Smith." "Smith" brought back some old memories. Bad ones. I buzzed "Owner" and waited. After thirty seconds I was about to buzz again, when I heard footsteps and the door opened about a foot. She was taller than Elle, spare in build, with gray streaks in her hair, but I could see the family resemblance.

"Mrs. Helgesen?"

"Yes?"

"My name is Max Grant, and I'd like to talk with you about your niece, Annette."

"You from the police?"

"No. I'm a private investigator."

"How you ... ? Oh, my sister."

"Elle. Yes."

She made a wry face, sighed, and then, standing to one side, opened the door for me to come in. She closed the door and then, without saying a word, walked down the hallway toward the back of the house. I followed like the caboose on a stacker in a rail yard. Our destination was the kitchen, and when we got there, she motioned toward the table.

"Have a seat. Coffee?"

"Thank you. Coffee would be nice. Black."

She poured two cups and sat at the table across from me. I took a sip. Obviously the number-one ingredient was oil used to spray on gravel roads.

I smiled. "Good coffee."

She smiled back. "I like it strong."

I suppressed an urge to say, "No shit, Dick Tracy." Instead, I cleared the tar from my throat and asked,

"When was the last time you saw or talked with Annette?"

She ignored the question. "My sister hired you?"

"Yes."

"I didn't know she had the money, or at least enough to hire a detective."

"She had enough."

"I can imagine how she got it."

"I didn't ask. Look, Mrs. Helgesen, I've been hired to find someone, and in order to do that, I need information. Aren't you interested in finding Annette?"

"Of course I'm interested."

"Then help me out. When was the last time you saw Annette?"

Without hesitation, she replied, "A week ago last Saturday. She was going out on a date. Some man picked her up in a fancy car."

"A week ago last Saturday. That would have been ..."

"The 16th."

"I took another sip and suppressed a shudder. "And today is the 28th. No word at all from her since then? No phone call?" I had noticed a phone on the kitchen counter.

"No, nothing."

"You reported her missing to the police?"

"Yes. The Tuesday after."

"Why did you wait three days? Was she in the habit of going off for a few days without letting you know?"

"No ... But the previous weekend, she left on Saturday and didn't return till Sunday evening. And it's not like she's a child: she's 22. But that was the first time she'd been gone for more than an evening. I was reluctant to report it to the police for fear they'd go to Columbia University looking for her, and she might lose her job over it. As it turned out, it was misplaced concern. They told me adults go missing all the time, and unless I suspected or could prove she had come to harm, they wouldn't spend much time looking for her. Oh, they didn't say it quite that way, but that's what they meant."

She offered more coffee, but my stomach rebelled, so I politely turned it down. "What the police told you is correct. They don't put much effort into looking for adults, and truth be told, not a hell of a lot more in looking for children unless they've been missing five days or more. The first time she was gone for a night— did the same fellow pick her up as last time?"

"No. No one picked her up the first time. She just said she was meeting someone. Didn't say who."

"Did you meet the fellow who picked her up in the car?"

"He came to the door and she introduced him as David. No last name."

It was most likely the David Braun that Elle had mentioned, but I didn't want to volunteer the name. Sometimes, when the person you're questioning thinks you already know more than they do, they clam up.

Thinking it doesn't hurt to grease the skids, I said, "I'll bet you're a good judge of people. What did you think of him?"

She paused, took another sip of road oil. "Well, I don't like to judge ..."

"Of course you don't. I don't either, but life experience and intuition are qualities you obviously have. I could tell the minute I met you that you were sophisticated and had good judgement." My only other thought at the moment was, "God is going to get you for this, Max."

Another sip. I almost winced, but kept myself under control as she said, "Well, I didn't like him. He was too smooth, too slick ... and jittery. Wanted to get going. No time for niceties or a moment's conversation. I want to say, slimy, but that's the wrong word and maybe too strong. But he was nicely dressed. A bit loud for my taste but clean. He wore a yellow sport coat with a pale yellow shirt and dark slacks."

"You're very observant, Mrs. Helgesen. How about his features? How tall was he?"

"Maybe five feet seven or eight, and medium build. Light and slightly wavy hair. Not blonde, but straw colored. Clean-shaven. I'm not very good at guessing ages, but I'd say he was about thirty."

"You certainly would make a good witness at a trial, ma'am."

"Goodness! I hope it doesn't come to that. Do you think this David had anything to do with Annette's disappearance?"

"It's too soon to tell, but I'd like to track him down and talk with him. Could I take a look at Annette's room?"

"I suppose it would be all right. It's just down the hallway. I rent to two boarders. They have rooms upstairs. Annette and I have bedrooms downstairs and a bath."

I followed her down the hallway toward the front door then into the second room on the right, next to the bath. The room was neat, tidy. Not spare, but not crowded either. There were a couple impressionist paintings on the wall. Copies, maybe, but I didn't look close enough to tell. There was a twin bed, bedside table, small writing desk, dresser, and closet. I wasn't interested in the clothes she wore. Didn't really know what the hell I was interested in, but just wanted to get a feel for the young woman. On the dresser was a framed photo of Annette with her mother that looked recent. Elle was right. Annette looked remarkably like a younger version of her mother, with a figure to match. I picked it up and asked.

"Yes, that was taken a couple months ago. Annette bought a Brownie flash camera and for a while was taking pictures of everything."

"Did she have a photo album?"

"She planned to get one but hadn't. She kept the photos in a small blue box. It must be here somewhere."

She opened the top drawer of the dresser, then the two drawers below it. No luck. She paused for a moment, thinking, then went to the closet. The box was on the top shelf. She took it down and handed it to me. I removed the lid then quickly began looking at the photos one by one. There were at least fifty, mostly pastoral or of scenes of the city. Several looked as though they'd been taken in a snow-covered Central Park. There was one of Annette, a close-up, and I asked if I could borrow it.

"Yes. Certainly, if it will help find her."

I slipped it into my inside coat pocket. "I'll return it to you. Is the camera here?"

Back to the closet. Behind where the box was kept was the camera and one undeveloped roll of film. She took them down and handed them to me.

I looked at the camera. There was a roll in it with several photos taken. "I'd like to borrow these as well."

She nodded. "Maybe there's a picture of that David on there."

"Maybe. We'll see."

We went back downstairs, and after politely turning down a refill of what she called coffee, I thanked her, left, and headed back to Eighth Avenue for a bus. I'd stop by Jacob Resnick's photographic studio on the way back to my office and ask him to develop the film for me.

FOUR

She was ice cold. Her teeth chattered and she shivered from head to toe. She was lying on a bed, eyes closed. Raising her head slightly, she tried to open her eyes, but they felt swollen and her lashes stuck together. She raised her right arm to wipe her eyes, but it simply fell to her face as if it belonged to someone else. Concentrate! Concentrate! Her hand moved to her eyes and rubbed. They opened ever so slightly and she looked down toward the foot of the bed. She was naked!

An ivory-colored blanket, lying on top of a silk sheet, was crumpled at the end of the bed, and she sat up quickly to retrieve it. Too quickly. Her head reeled, and that's when the stomach pain and cramps struck. She snatched the blanket, pulled it up as far as her breasts then fell back, disoriented and dizzy. She was going to be sick. Aloud, she moaned, "Oh, God, I don't want to be sick!" She rolled to her side and vomited, a greenish-yellow vomit. A vile, sour smell rolled up from the floor, enveloped her, and she retched again, but this time, nothing. She rolled onto her back, barely seeing the ceiling as tears streamed from her eyes.

The room was small, about ten by twelve, but reasonably well appointed with a double bed, partial carpet, and curtains on the one window. The window was barred. There was a closet with shelves just to the left of the door, and a small table with a padded office chair in the corner opposite.

She coughed, and as she did, a bit of urine escaped, wetting herself. It burned, and vague, dreamlike memories invaded her thoughts. Men. A lot of them. A lot of them pressing down on her, lifting her legs, rolling her over ... Then needles—the rush after a shot of heroin to the inside of her thigh, and she would feel on top of the world. But quickly, her mind would become slow and fuzzy, somewhere between being asleep and awake. The door would open, a man would come in and begin to undress, and she didn't care ...

She glanced to her left to a small, curtained-off area. Behind it was a toilet and washbasin. Shuffling, wrapped in the blanket, she made it to the toilet, then to the washbasin where she splashed warm water on her face. After she dried her face, she ran hot water on a washrag, squeezed it out, folded it, and pressed it between her legs. It burned. God, how it burned! There was a spray bottle of cheap perfume on the back of the toilet and she used it, if for no other reason than to rid herself of the smell of vomit that lingered.

Looking in the cabinet mirror on the wall above the basin, she saw herself, an image she didn't recognize. Aloud, she asked, "Who are you?" Then, almost a murmur, "What are you?" The answer to both questions, she knew: Annette Fouchet, a heroin addict and whore.

A terrycloth bathrobe hung on a clothes hook next to the toilet, and she slipped it on before going back to the bed. She sat, glanced down at the small puddle of vomit and knew she'd have to clean it up. There was a bucket and sponge next to the toilet. She'd get to it in a few minutes, but she wanted to think, to think about how she'd come to this. As her mind began to clear, she became aware of two things: first was that she needed a fix—badly! Second, that she would probably die here, wherever *here* was.

FIVE

I took a bus back across the river to Brooklyn, transferred, then transferred again to one that took me north on Ninety-eighth Street to Livonia. Jake Resnick's shop was on the far western edge of Brownsville, a predominantly Jewish district in Brooklyn, and if not the toughest section of the city, it's certainly in the top three. Home of Murder Incorporated and such notable, if unpleasant, personalities as Bugsy Siegel, Meyer Lansky, and Dutch Schultz, it has a fearsome reputation. Siegel and Lansky are still above ground but Schultz, whose real name was Arthur Flegenheimer, was hammered by the mob. Hitman Charlie Workman shot him while he was taking a leak in the restroom of the Palace Chop House in Newark, New Jersey. Workman hit what he was aiming at. Schultz probably didn't.

The bell above the door tinkled as I walked into Jake's shop. He was sitting at his desk, lighting a pipe, and took a few puffs before asking, "So, what are you doing here, stranger?"

"Yeah, it's been a while."

"About two weeks. Wanna play chess?"

"Not today."

"Bring bourbon?"

"Not today."

"What good are you?"

"Not much, I guess. At least not today."

"Well ... no chess, no bourbon. You must want something. Have a seat. Want some tobacco? You did bring a pipe with you, didn't you?"

I took a seat in the chair beside his desk and fished my pipe from my coat pocket. "Yeah, the large Peterson you talked me into buying about a month ago."

"Good smoke?"

"One of my best."

He took a blue tin from his desk drawer and handed it to me. "Try this. Edgeworth Sliced. Naturally sweet. You'll like it."

"I do like it. You gave me some a few months ago—back in December, I think." I took a couple tobacco slices, crumpled them up, stuffed them in the bowl of my pipe, and lit up.

"So, Max, you want something?"

"I need some copies made of a photograph, and I need some film developed." I took the photo of Annette out of my pocket, handed it to Jake, and set the film roll and camera on the desk.

"When do you need them?"

"Soon as possible."

"I shouldn't have asked." He picked up the camera and turned it over. "Six pictures taken. You're getting smart in your old age, Max."

"Why is that?"

"Because you didn't open the camera to take the film out. Would have ruined at least two of the photos, maybe all." He looked at the photo of Annette. "Pretty girl. Friend of yours?"

"No. Missing."

"Another one?"

"Yeah, finding missing women is getting to be a habit with us."

"How many copies of the photo?"

"Six should do it."

"I have to take a photo of the photo. You'll lose a bit of definition but not enough for the average person to notice. I'll have your six copies in a half hour or so, but the others from the roll and camera won't be ready till tomorrow morning. I have another job to complete this afternoon. Go next door to the diner and get yourself some coffee and a rugelach, maybe a couple."

"What's a rugelach?"

"A rolled pastry. Get the chocolate. They're to die for."

Jake was right. The pastries were delicious. I ate two, thought about a third, nixed it, but got four to take back to the office for Pepper. She could take them home as an after-dinner treat for her and Bo.

While sipping my coffee, I leafed through a copy of a newspaper someone had left behind. There was a report that the German American Bund is still going strong and perhaps gaining strength after their huge rally in Madison Square Garden the previous year. They held a recent mass meeting at Camp Norland in New Jersey led by their leader, Wilhelm Kunze, who is actually from Manhattan. There was also a rumored connection between the Bund and the Ku Klux Klan, and talk of a combined rally in the future. Made sense to me: both organizations hated anyone who disagreed with them. The world is full of idiots, and those two organizations seem to have cornered the market.

And there was an interesting report from London that made *no* sense to me:

A strong force from the Home Fleet has been cruising in northern waters to provide support for the Norwegian Convoys and the Northern Patrol. On the 22nd and 23rd March a sweep into the Skagerrak was carried out by light forces, with the object of intercepting German merchant shipping. None was met with by these forces.

Some success was achieved by our submarines working in these waters ... and the consequent interruption of the flow of German merchant shipping may account, in part, for the lack of success by our light forces.

I tried to figure out how "some success" and "consequent interruption" equaled "lack of success," but gave up. I'll never understand the British. Hopefully, the Germans won't, either.

Jake was sitting at his desk drinking something from a cup: coffee, bourbon, or both. As I sat down, my eyes and nose told me it was both.

"Want some sweetened coffee, Max?"

"Love some, but I have to go back to the office, and Pepper would send me to my room if I came in smelling ripe. I'll try to make it some evening in a week or so for some chess and high-test coffee. I'll bring the high test."

"What brand high test?"

"Getting picky in your old age?"

"Just like to plan ahead—something to look forward to."

"Old Forester suit you? I have an unopened bottle."

"Yep, that'll work." Jake pointed to an envelope. "Your copies and the original are in there. Copies came out looking good. Hard to tell from the original. I put a small check mark in pencil on the back of the original."

I took them out of the envelope and spread them on the desk. To my untrained eye, they all looked the same. "Great job, Jake. What time tomorrow morning for the others?"

"Any time after ten. You want one set, or two?"

"Two. If I need more, I'll come back."

"I'll keep the negatives. Just call me."

"Hell, Jake, I didn't know you had a phone." I looked around and didn't see one.

He opened the bottom desk drawer and there it was. "Got it a couple weeks ago."

"Why do you keep it in the drawer?"

"Funny thing about phones—when they ring, ya just gotta answer them. In the drawer, I don't hear it when I'm in the darkroom."

I gathered up the photos, put them in the envelope, and stood. "Thanks for the favor, Jake. I'll see you in the morning."

I walked to Ninety-eighth Street, crossed to the other side, and while waiting on a bus, did some window-shopping at a small cutlery shop a few feet from the bus stop. They had the usual kitchen assortment displayed, along with some Victorinox multipurpose knives similar to the one I carried. I only use mine to clean my fingernails and open envelopes, but it also had scissors, a screwdriver, and a can opener that I'd never used but could come in handy in a pinch. The shop also had a nice selection of switchblade knives, also known as pushbutton or flick knives. Looking at the switchblades reminded me of an incident I'd seen several weeks earlier.

I'd ambled out of Jimmy's Bar in lower Manhattan about midnight and had gone about a half block when I heard two fellows arguing just inside the entrance to an alley. I stopped at the edge of the alley and leaned against a building—I have a thing about alleys, but that's another story—listening to what I assumed were a couple drunks getting ready to have a go at each other, a la Lewis and Galento in June of the previous year. I was right about that part, but it wasn't with fists; it was with knives. As I watched, the bigger of the two pulled a knife and I saw it flick open, the blade flashing in the glare from an overhead streetlight. He moved into a crouch, tossing the switchblade from hand to hand. The smaller fellow backed up a couple paces, pulled a large clasp knife from his coat pocket, opened it, and simply stood there.

Now, in the movies, we see sword fights with a lot of flashing blade against blade that seems to go on for a long time. It's Hollywood. The good guys against the bad guys. In reality, that probably isn't true, and in knife fights, it certainly isn't. Knife fights are over quickly, and there's nothing Hollywood about it.

The big fellow moved in, grinning, still passing his switchblade from hand to hand, and then the smaller fellow moved so fast I hardly caught it. He stepped forward and made two rapid thrusts. The first caught the big guy's knife midair and flipped it ten feet away. The second slammed his blade into his opponent high in the belly. They seemed frozen in time. Neither moved. Then, with a muffled groan, the big guy slowly fell backward away from the knife, which slid easily out of his stomach. The smaller fellow reached down, wiped his blade on the big guy's pants, folded it and put it back in his pocket before turning in my direction to walk out of the alley. As he came closer, I moved away from the wall. He stopped about ten feet away and shrugged. I shrugged back. He went his way, and I went back to Jimmy's. After one bourbon and one phone call to the cops, in that order, I went home.

Pepper was sitting at her desk, a bottle of Coke within reach, and reading a newspaper when I walked in the door to our office. She reached into her purse and took out an envelope.

"Well, boss, it's real."

"How much real?"

"To the jeweler, 350 bucks, but he said to a private buyer, maybe 150 more."

"What's our bank account look like?"

"We're solvent. More than solvent. With the two insurance cases we wrapped up last month and the jewelry recovery from that nasty Bergan divorce, we probably have at least ten months of expenses covered. That Bergan case paid a ten percent recovery fee."

"Refresh my memory."

"Twelve thousand seven hundred."

"Plus the insurance fees."

"Yeah, plus the insurance fees. Why? Thinking of going to Europe for the summer?"

"No, just thinking ... All right. Put the gem in the floor safe for now. We'll cash it when we need to."

I set the sack I was carrying on her desk. "Dessert for you and Bo after dinner tonight. Something sweet and chocolaty."

She opened the sack and looked. "Bo usually has something else in mind for dessert, but I'll fend him off and have the rugelach."

I just looked at her, decided to skip Bo, and asked, "How is it you know rugelach at a glance?"

"I roomed with a girl named Ruth Berman for two semesters in college. She got a package from home every month that was almost always pastries. Rugelach was a regular."

"I should've known." I took the envelope that held the photos of Annette from my pocket and handed it to Pepper. "That's the woman we're looking for."

She opened the envelope and spread the photos on her desk. "Pretty girl, and definitely looks like Mama. Why so many copies?"

"I'm not sure where this case is headed yet. We may need help looking for her, and whoever we hire will have to have a copy. I may want to give one to Sergeant Belden as well."

Belden, a member of New York's finest, was a good cop but could be a prick of the first order. We got along, sometimes even shared information, but he didn't have much regard for private investigators. I had to admit, though, he did help with the Sarah Bennett investigation, providing some good advice, and even gave me some helpful information afterward. At least I was no longer on his shit list.

She put the photos back in the envelope, then asked, "Any good information from the sister, Anna Helgesen?"

"Some, and some additional snapshots as well. Jake Resnick is going to develop the film. He'll have them ready tomorrow morning. There was a boyfriend, someone with enough money to own a car and dress well. She only knew him as David, but it was probably the David Braun mentioned by Elle. Mrs. Helgesen was not very forthcoming. Getting information was like pulling teeth, but she did let me see Annette's bedroom. No leads other than Braun, and not much of interest except for the camera and photos. Oh—one more thing. If you ever have occasion to visit her place, don't accept the offer of coffee."

"Bad?"

"Words can't describe, though 'tar' comes close."

"I'll remember. By the way, your nearest and dearest phoned."

"Ari?"

"Unless you have more than one nearest and dearest I don't know about."

"Couldn't afford it. Leave a message?"

"Yeah. She won't be home till after seven. She'll expect you for dinner about eight."

"She's taking a lot for granted. What if I have other plans?"

Pepper looked at me with a hint of a smile on her face. "What? You planning on sleeping alone tonight?"

I managed a smirk, but no reply to the question. Instead, I said, "I wonder if there's some way to get hold of Ari at work without making it sound like some emergency."

"Maybe. I can try if you like."

"Sure. Go ahead." I stood in the doorway to my office and filled my pipe while she looked in the phone directory. Finding the number she wanted, she dialed then mouthed to me, "Saks Personnel."

"Hello, who's speaking, please? ... Well, Miss Price, this is Miss Brown of Grant Perfume Distributors. Could I leave a message for one of your managers? ... That's very kind of you. Please ask Miss Ariella Blumfeld to phone at her earliest convenience. She has our number. Tell her to ask for Mr. Grant. ... Thank you, Miss Price. We appreciate it."

Listening, I had forgotten to light my pipe. "Pepper, you're a wonder. When was the last time you had a raise?"

"Let's see. Been a while, but me and Bo took a bubble bath this morning and he sure got a raise ..."

I damn near swallowed my pipe stem. I didn't say a word. Walked into my office, stopped at my desk, lit my pipe, set it in the ashtray, and returned to the door. "Five bucks."

"Five bucks?"

"A week. Maybe you can buy a few blocks of ice to put in the tub."

"Wouldn't make any difference. They'd melt too quick."

I was trying to keep a straight face. "I give up." And with that, I returned to my desk, sat, and relit my pipe.

I doubt if there's any boss-employee relationship in the city like ours. Well, in a sense, she's more partner than employee, but on occasion, our conversations are more like those of estranged but familiar lovers. If someone came through the door during one of those exchanges, I'd have some explaining to do. If that ever does happen, I pray it isn't Bo. I have no desire to do a three-story swan dive from my office window.

"Hey, Pepper, any fresh coffee?"

"About a half hour ago."

"Great. Thanks." I got up, walked to Pepper's domain, poured myself a cup, and returned to my desk. A bourbon sounded better, but during the day, I tend to stick with coffee.

I had some thinking to do. It just seemed strange to me that a girl like Annette—decent relationship with her mother, fair relationship with her aunt, and good job—would simply disappear of her own free will. That opened the door to several possibilities: eloping with boyfriend, murder, rape-murder, kidnapping ... no, not kidnapping, at least not for money, and there'd been no demand. At least no demand to her aunt. That thought opened another door. What if someone knew Elle had gems worth a lot of money but didn't know how or where to get in touch with her? Unlikely, but I put it on the back burner to ask Elle if she knew of anyone asking about her in the neighborhood where she'd been staying.

The phone rang and Pepper picked it up in her office. Thinking it might be Ari, my hand hovered over my phone. It wasn't. I couldn't make out all that was said, but I did get the end of the conversation. "All right, I'll tell him. Thank you."

Pepper came into my office and handed me a slip of paper. "That was Elle. She has a bed-sitting room on Troy Avenue just south of Snyder here in Brooklyn. East Flatbush, actually. Last house on the left as you walk toward the cemetery. She said it's eight bucks a week and there's a phone in the hallway. The number's on that paper, but she also said the place is pretty much deserted during the day, so if you phone, let it ring. If she's there, she'll get it."

"How'd she sound?"

"Like she'd used a couple bucks for a bottle."

"Shit! We don't need a drunk for a client, though I should have guessed as much. Granted, with as much practice as she's had, she can probably hold her liquor, but I may have more questions for her and don't need fuzzy answers."

Regis McCafferty

"We can always drop the case."

"Don't tempt me."

"Ah, you ain't going to do that, boss. Being on the hunt for someone is your idea of fun."

"Some fun!" But I was grinning. Pepper was right ... as usual.

SIX

The afternoon was quiet except for a phone call while I was in the men's room—a men's room when a man is in it, a ladies' room when a woman is in it. I hurried the process because I thought it might be Ariella, but I was wrong. As I came into my office, I heard Pepper say, "I'll be sure to pass that information on to Mr. Grant. Thank you for calling."

A sip of cold coffee and a lit pipe later, Pepper came into my office carrying a notepad, and sat down in the chair next to my desk. "That was Mr. Fraley of Fraley and Associates. Remember him? Back in December, Fraley had us look into the theft of some securities by a fellow named Arthur Schmidt. Based on the best information we had at the time, we assumed Schmidt had gone to New Mexico or Arizona, but instead of sending me and Bo out there to look for him, you had an investigator in New Mexico take over the job. No trace of Schmidt after two weeks of looking." She was smiling. "Bo still holds a grudge over that. He was looking forward to some real Mexican food in Santa Fe."

"Sorry, but I needed you here. What did Fraley have to say?"

"Schmidt was arrested day before yesterday. All those New Mexico and Arizona brochures he had in his desk were a blind. He'd changed his name to Albert Shear and simply moved about ten blocks from Lexington at 108th Street to 119th Street, about a half block from Holy Rosary church."

"Same initials anyway, AS. Probably spent time in church praying they wouldn't find him. How did they?"

"A woman who works for Fraley, a widow named Bennati, lives a couple blocks away from Holy Rosary on Pleasant Street. She went to a local late night deli for some milk and bread and spotted him there. He'd grown a beard, but she recognized him. He didn't see her. The following morning, she told Fraley, and he contacted the FBI. It took them two days to run him down."

I tamped my pipe and set it in the ashtray. "And the loot?"

"He still had the entire forty thousand. He'd apparently saved enough from his salary to live on for a year or more, and was waiting for things to cool off."

"Forty thousand? I thought Fraley told us originally it was twenty thousand."

"Yeah, he did, but it seems Schmidt was also an expert at creative bookkeeping, and hid some sort of bank transfer that showed up later. The FBI agent said he was a cautious man and had planned to sell them to a fence for 50 cents on the dollar. He was afraid of trying to cash them in, himself."

"He's talking, then."

"Saw no reason not to, I guess."

"Could be more to it. There was nothing in the newspapers about the theft at the time. No publicity and details of how he went about doing it might be worth a lesser charge to Fraley and the FBI. He probably cut a deal." I was about to say something else, something undoubtedly innocuous, when the phone rang. I picked it up.

"Grant Investigations."

"Mr. Grant, this is Miss Blumfeld of Saks. Miss Price said you phoned."

"You must be in a room full of people, Ari."

"Yes, that's correct."

"I understand. I need information on an employee of Saks, a David Braun. Maybe a past employee. Anything you can get, including gossip. Think you can do that?"

"Yes, I'm sure we'd be interested in your perfumes, Mr. Grant. May we set up an appointment?"

"How about tonight ... in bed ... after dinner?" Pepper, stifling a laugh, stood and walked to her office.

"That would be fine, Mr. Grant. We'll see you then."

I lifted my pipe from the ashtray, lit it, and wandered to Pepper's domain. She was looking at a newspaper but still had a smile on her face. Without looking up, she said, "Why bother with dinner? Seems like a waste of time."

"By then, I'll want something to eat."

She looked up, still smiling. Didn't say a word.

I stared for a few seconds, connecting the dots. "I swear, Pepper, you have a one-track mind. I'll bet Bo has to fend you off with a big stick."

"Oh, he gotta big stick, all right."

"I quit. What are you reading?"

"A copy of the *Philadelphia Inquirer* someone left on the bus. It's a few days old."

"Anything interesting?"

"Mrs. Roosevelt is involved with some delivery boys' strike, and the French have a new government ... well, a new cabinet, anyway."

"Same old stuff."

"How would you know? You never read the newspaper."

"Rarely. But I do listen to the radio."

"I didn't know they did the news on the Jack Benny program."

"I don't know either, but they broadcast the news just before 'The Shadow.' There's five minutes of news just before they begin with, 'who knows what evil lurks in the hearts of men? The shadow knows!' followed by that sinister laugh." I laughed.

"My god, Max, you sound just like him."

"Been practicing. It's just a couple hours shy of quitting time. Why don't you take the rest of the afternoon off. I'm going to be here for a while anyway."

"You don't have to say that twice, boss. I can get home early enough to fix a nice dinner for bo. I'll leave the newspaper for you. It has a comics section, in case you get bored."

"Get out of here! Oh, and tell Bo I said hello." I was smiling. Figured it was smart to stay on the good side of that mountain on two legs.

After Pepper left, I washed the coffee cups in the bathroom, set them on a towel next to the coffee pot, walked to my stash cabinet, poured myself a couple ounces of bourbon, and went to my desk.

After a sip and relighting my pipe, I thought about the case, what little there was to think about. Other than the fact that Annette had disappeared, there was nothing solid to go on. She could stay missing, turn up at her aunt's today, or wash up on the banks of the hudson. I picked up the piece of paper with Elle's phone number on it and dialed. It was answered on the ninth ring.

"Hello?"

"Elle?"

"Tha's me. Who's this?" She wasn't sloshed, but Pepper had been right about the booze.

"Max Grant."

"Oh ... Mr. Grant ... Find out anything?"

I was tempted to say no and hang up, but I'm a nice guy—most of the time. "For one thing, your stone is good. Worth a couple weeks' work, at any rate."

"Tha's nice. Toll you it was."

"I also met with your sister." Elle didn't say anything, so I went on. "She didn't have much that was helpful, but she did confirm that Annette was dating David Braun. And she had some recent photos and undeveloped film, plus a partial roll still in the camera. I'm having that developed and will pick up the pictures tomorrow. I'm hoping it will give us a lead."

More silence. Then: "So ... you don' have shit."

"No, but it's only been a day, and we're working on a couple other angles. I do have two questions."

"Yeah?"

"Have you heard of anyone that's been looking for you, maybe when you were in the Bowery, or wherever you were living?"

Pause. Trolling through the fog of memory. "No ... Why?"

"Just wondering. If someone knew you had those gemstones ..." I stopped to let her think it through— make her work for it.

She connected, and the question sobered her up some. "You mean someone might take Annette to get the stones?"

"Yeah, that's a possibility."

"No one knows I have them except you and two separate jewelers I sold stones to, one each."

I took a sip of bourbon. "Probably rules that out, then."

"What's the second question?"

"Did you ever drink any of your sister's coffee?"

"Oh, Jesus! You didn't, did you?"

"Yeah, 'bout a cup."

"She mixes chicory half and half with coffee, then puts double the normal amount in the pot and lets it perc for about twenty minutes or more. Stay close to a bathroom. That stuff will work on you."

"Thanks for the advice. I'll be in touch. And hey—go slow on the booze, huh?"

"Yeah ... Guess I'd better."

I finished off the rest of the bourbon in my glass, rinsed it out, and put it away. I had some time to kill, but sticking around the office was getting stale so I decided to walk to the local tobacconist's to do some window-shopping.

But first, I had to measure the space inside my stash cabinet. I think the cabinet had originally been a built-in bookcase, but long before my time, someone had put doors on it and turned it into storage space. Outside, it was about three feet high by four feet wide, and inside, just slightly smaller and ten inches deep. I didn't have much in it—several bottles of booze, a couple packs of luckys, three jars of pipe tobacco, and nine pipes. Well, nine pipes, less the couple I usually had on my desk or in my pocket. But the pipes lay on a folded towel, and since my pipe smoking had become a regular habit, I wanted to get a rack to store my pipes in. I took a ruler from my desk and measured the space between the two shelves that gave me three levels of storage. Roughly fourteen, twelve, and ten inches, bottom to top. Plenty of room. I picked up my pipe and tobacco pouch, went to the coat rack, and slipped on my newsboy cap and jacket. I paused to look around the office to see if I was forgetting anything. Nope.

It was a nice day for a change, cool, but the sun was shining. The radio weather report had predicted rain, but none had materialized as yet. As I walked out the front door of the building, I stopped, lit my pipe, and savored the flavor and aroma of the tobacco. Unlike the acrid cigarettes I'd given up some months ago, the taste and aroma of the pipe was nut-like and slightly sweet.

I normally use a tobacconist in the Brownsville area of Brooklyn, about a half block from Jake's place, but wanted to get back to my office before heading out to Ariella's apartment. Doogan's, near Jake's, is small store, warm, and filled with the aroma of cigars and pipe tobacco. The owner is Michael Doogan, a mick who is affectionately known as Mick. In his fifties, short, squat, red-faced and with red hair, he's always ready with a smile and a joke, usually Irish.

The shop I headed for was larger than Mick's and had more in the way of stock, but didn't have the warm atmosphere of Doogan's. No matter. I knew they had pipe racks because I'd seen them in the window.

It was a short walk of little more than a block and a shorter visit to the tobacco shop. As I passed in front of the shop, headed for the door, I saw the rack I wanted. It would hold fourteen pipes and I figured that would be enough for now. I stepped inside, caught the eye of the clerk, pointed out the rack I wanted, and then looked at brands of tobacco. I hadn't smoked Sir Walter Raleigh tobacco before, so I bought two pouches and was out the door in less than five minutes. I should have stayed a minute longer.

As I came out the door, a fellow in one helluva hurry slammed into me, knocking the package out of my hand onto the sidewalk, and throwing me against an elderly woman who was going the other way. She didn't fall but brushed her shoulder against the building and kept on going.

I didn't think it was my fault but said to the guy, "Excuse me."

"Why don't you watch where you're going, you dumb son of a bitch." He made it a statement, not a question.

"I said 'excuse me.' But if you hadn't been barreling along here, not paying any attention to others on the sidewalk, this wouldn't have happened."

He took a couple steps toward me like he was going to eat me up. Now, I'm a bit under six feet and about 175 pounds. This dolt was at least three inches shorter and better than thirty pounds lighter. When he got within arm's reach, he started to mouth off again. I didn't wait for him to finish. On a whim, I slapped him. Hard. Back and forth, both sides of his face. He stopped, stock still, a look of disbelief on his face. Now I was pissed. I said, "Sonny, you'd best run along before you really get hurt."

I took a step toward him and that's what he did— turned and ran. At about thirty feet, he glanced over his shoulder, saw I wasn't following, and slowed to a fast walk. I picked up my package, looked to make sure the rack was intact, and walked back to my building.

Back in my office, I put the rack in my cabinet and placed seven pipes in it. Half-filled, the rack looked bare, so I spaced the pipes, one every other slot. Looked better.

With time to kill before going to Ari's, I decided to take a shower. The bath contains a recently installed shower stall, sink, toilet, and small closet. Sufficient for my needs and occasional use by others. I'd showered in the morning, but it's always nice to smell fresh when meeting your favorite woman. Aside from that, I'd noticed in the morning that my mustache needed trimmed, so I locked the doors to the office and got with it.

SEVEN

David Braun sat in his car nursing a grudge and a pint bottle of whiskey wrapped in a paper sack. Both his cheeks were still red and the left one was sore to the touch. Slapped! He couldn't believe he'd been slapped like some little kid who had misbehaved. And in public! All those people watching. Then he ran in fear. He tried to mollify his feelings by telling himself it was the prudent thing to do, not draw more attention to himself, but he knew some of the red on his cheeks was embarrassment. "If I have a gun on me next time I see that son of a bitch—" he mumbled. He had several handguns and decided he'd begin carrying one. In any case, given the business he was in, it was probably a good idea.

He opened the glove compartment, took out a small mirror, and looked at his face. The red on his cheeks was fading. Time to get back to business. Time to add another filly to his stable. Marcia was good. Marcia was ready. Marcia was hooked. She loved coke. She loved horse. And she loved sex. This could be a long-term relationship. She was not particularly attractive, but simply inviting. She oozed sensuality. She would stand, feet planted solidly, legs parted, pelvis pushed slightly forward, and would attract every man who saw her from a half city block away.

As he stepped out of his car, he paused. The sack was resting against the transmission hump, and the neck of the whiskey bottle was poking out about two inches. Better get that out of sight, he thought. No sense inviting an inquisitive cop to start asking questions. Not that he'd ever seen a cop on this street, but the way his luck was running ... He slid back into his car, made sure the cork was tight in the neck, and pulled the sack over the top of the bottle before sliding it under the seat.

Marcia's apartment was first floor, rear, which was convenient because she had her own entrance. No pushing buzzers at the mailbox panel in the front alcove and taking a chance on getting the landlady if Marcia wasn't in. He walked up the three front steps then followed the narrow concrete path to the back of the house.

They met while he still worked at Saks, dated a while, and tested her mattress on numerous occasions, but had drifted apart after a couple months. He reconnected with her intentionally after several months when he realized he needed a couple more girls for his brothel. She was streetwise, an intermittent user of horse and coke, and though she'd never said so, he guessed she wasn't above trading sex for drugs. It had taken six weeks of supplying cheap heroin to get her hooked to the point where she was a daily user. She was still working for Saks, though he suspected not for long. She was taking off more days than she was there, and if she disappeared, they'd never miss her: she had no relatives in the city or anywhere else he knew of. Her father died when she was eleven, drunk in some gutter somewhere, and her mother died in an accident some seven years later.

No, no one would miss her, except maybe her landlady when the rent was due. Marcia had come to New York from Savannah, Georgia, when she was nineteen years old, with stars in her eyes and dreams of a career on stage. The dreams and stars were long gone. She was now in her late twenties, maybe even thirty, but had an almost little-girl-like quality that could be misleading at times. She had a couple traits he didn't care for but would overlook for now: she was smart, a thinker, and she could sometimes be stubborn to the point of being aggressive. But she was prime ass for his needs, and that faint, soft southern accent was a nice come-on.

He knocked on the door, waited, and was about to knock again when it opened. He stepped in and she gave him a quick kiss on the lips. She smelled of a light perfume and maybe gin, he couldn't be sure, but what he did notice were the tiny beads of sweat on her forehead and upper lip, her eyes never resting on him or any other place in the kitchen, always darting to and fro. Her movements were a bit jerky as she stepped to the stove for the coffee pot. She was in need of a fix.

She lifted the pot. "Coffee, honey?"

"Yeah, 'bout half a cup."

She took a cup from one of the cup hooks above the sink, almost dropped it, and then, with two hands, placed it on the table before slopping almost a full cup of coffee in it.

As she set the pot down, he asked, "Need some help?"

She turned. "What do you mean?"

"You know what I mean."

"Yeah ... Need ... Need some . . ."

He took a small zippered leather case from his coat pocket, just large enough for two vials and a needle, and handed it to her.

She took it, smiled thanks, a crooked smile, said, "Back in a minute," and hurried out of the kitchen.

He took a sip of coffee. Lousy. He should have brought the whiskey from the car to sweeten it up. He knew the only booze Marcia had in her place was gin, and he couldn't stand the stuff. He stood, walked to the mirror mounted like a small picture on the pantry door, and looked at his face. The redness was almost gone. He became angry again thinking about the incident, but then shrugged his shoulders. Someday, he might have a chance to pay the bastard back, and he let it go at that.

Marcia came back in the kitchen, calmer, more in control, and handed him back his case.

As he took it, he asked, "One or two?"

"Just one vial ... for now. Want to go have a bite to eat ... or go to bed?"

"Neither at the moment. You still working?"

"No. Got laid off."

"You mean fired."

"Yeah—fired. Couldn't keep it together without a fix and couldn't get a fix when I needed it, so I drank on the job. Didn't take 'em long to find that out."

"What are you going to do?"

She pulled a chair out from the table and sat. "I don't know."

She looked as though she were on the verge of tears. He couldn't stand that shit, but instead of offering words of comfort about her job, he asked, "How would you like to go to a place where you could get a steady supply of horse and they'd take care of you? Room, food, whatever you need."

"What would I have to do?"

"What you do best."

She looked at him, not quite understanding. Then it dawned on her. "No ... I couldn't ... I couldn't."

They were always like this, he thought, but the need for the drug soon overcame reluctance and morals. Aloud, he said, "Well, suit yourself, Marcia, but I can't continue to supply you beyond today. This is the last of it. You'll have to find some other source."

Now she was crying. "You can't do that to me. I'm hooked. You got me hooked, goddamn it!"

Time for lies. He cleared his throat. "I do understand, but my sources are drying up. It took me three hours this morning just to connect for the horse you just shot up. At this rate, it may be a week, or even a month, before I get more."

"God! Jesus! I can't go a week or a month! I can't go a day!"

He slowly stood as if he were getting ready to leave. Time for the pitch. "There's this woman I know down near the docks. She seems to have a steady supply. Must come in on some ships. She won't sell to me, but provides it for her girls. Coke, too. Her name is Bertha. I think you'd like her. That's all I can do for you."

She stood, walked to the sink, and dried her tears with a dish towel before turning to him. "I can't, David. That would make me a slut, a whore!"

He was tempted to tell her that's what she was already, but business was business. "No, it wouldn't, Marcia. You'd still be yourself. No one would know but you and Bertha, and you'd have what you need when you need it. Think about it and I'll come back next week."

"No! Don't go! Please don't go!"

There was a battle going on inside her. A mental battle, for sure, but also a physical one. The heroin had calmed her, but the thought of becoming a prostitute for the drug had riled her. She opened the cupboard above the sink and took down a glass and bottle of gin. She uncorked it, poured about four ounces in the glass, and drank it down. She brought bottle and glass to the table and sat for a moment without saying anything.

He understood. It was the game. Same game every time but with slightly different variations, slightly different reactions. And the game always ended the same way—a one-way trip to meet Bertha.

She poured a couple more ounces in her glass, sipped, and asked, "Should I pack a bag?"

EIGHT

Ari's apartment was on Hinsdale between Dumont and Blake, one bus transfer to a short trolley ride from my place, usually less than 30 minutes. I stepped off the trolley, lit my pipe, and walked north on Hinsdale the half block to the apartment house where I rang the buzzer for 2B.

Ari's voice came over the speaker. "If you're selling carpet, I don't need any."

I leaned close to the speaker. "I'm not selling carpet ... I'm here to clean yours."

She laughed. "In that case, come on up." The door clicked and unlocked.

She was at the door of her apartment, waiting. We'd been dating for several months but there were still times when she simply took my breath away. She was tall at about five feet seven, straw blonde, early thirties, and had a striking figure. She was wearing a pale green A-line dress with white pumps that matched the single strand of pearls at her neck. I stopped at the top of the stairs and stared.

She asked, "What?"

"I just love you, that's all."

"Oh—that's all, huh? Well, come on in, Mr. Carpet Cleaner."

I stepped in, closed the door behind me with my foot, embraced her, and we kissed. Passion and promise.

She moved away but still held my hand. "Hungry?"

"Yes, but more interested in carpet cleaning."

"Nope. After dinner and dessert."

"Dessert?"

"Cherry cobbler and ice cream."

"I'm going to get fat, Ari."

Laughing as she walked to the kitchen, she said over her shoulder, "You'll burn it off cleaning my carpet. Have a seat and light your pipe. I'll get you a glass of wine."

Like a good lad, I did as told. I sat, lit my pipe, and then looked at one of the magazines sitting on the end table next to the couch. It was the March 2nd issue of *Argosy* that I suspect she'd bought for me, though I hadn't seen it on my last visit. My last visit was late, and she greeted me at the door in a nightie. I had other things on my mind than magazines.

On the *Argosy* cover was an illustration of a handsome fellow knocking out a member of the German Bund who was holding a large dagger. The caption to the side of the picture read, *Smooth Kyle Returns! To beat the Bund and smash the Swastika to make America safe for America.* Underneath was the story title, "The Sun Sets at 5," by Borden Chase.

I had just turned to the story page when she came in with two glasses of white wine and sat beside me. She took a sip. "Dinner in ten minutes."

"Something smells good."

"Pork chops, home fries with shallots, and French bread. While we're waiting, do you want to hear about David Braun?"

"Anything interesting?"

"Depends. I don't know what you're looking for or why, but what I learned this afternoon is that he's a scumbag of the first order. He's no longer with Saks. Quit a few months ago, probably just ahead of being fired for absenteeism. But it was his personal relationships with several women that were talked about. Love 'em and leave 'em seemed to be his primary activity, or better put, love 'em and they leave.

"I did some checking with a friend of mine in Personnel. Braun was with us for ten months. Started working nights in Stock but transferred to Men's after two months. In that time, he dated four women who worked for us. None of them are still with Saks, though the last one just left a couple days ago. She was fired for drinking on the job and calling in sick one or two days a week. Two just kind of disappeared—simply stopped showing up for work. No notice or anything. Rumor, probably more than rumor, was that he dealt in drugs and got the women hooked."

"Would one of those women be Annette Fouchet?"

"I don't know. I mean, I knew her, but I don't know if she dated Braun. She was fluent in French and had an opportunity to take a position as an interpreter at Columbia University. She worked a two-week notice and left. That was several months ago. I can find out if she dated him."

"That won't be necessary. She did."

"Something you're working on?"

"She's missing."

Ari picked up her glass and stood. "Let's talk more in the kitchen. Dinner should be ready in a couple minutes."

The kitchen was warm and cozy, and dinner, delicious. We dropped the subject of David Braun temporarily and talked about the war in Europe. Ari kept herself more up to date on the war than I did, but being Jewish, she had a personal interest. She'd been born in Coburg, Germany, in Bavaria, but her parents had been killed in a train accident when she was very young. She immigrated to the States with relatives, and a younger brother had come with her. He, however, was currently in prison for stupidity, but that's another story.

We talked about Hitler's invasion of Poland from the west, Stalin's invasion of Poland from the east, and the rumors that both were executing Polish Jews or putting them in labor camps. It appeared to be a done deal that Germany would invade Denmark and Norway soon.

Ari set the dinner plates in the sink and took cherry cobbler out of the oven. I was amazed and asked, "Did you fix that, too, after you got home?"

She laughed. "No, I bought it, but put it in the oven to warm so the ice cream would melt on it a bit."

A moment later, she set a large slice of cobbler with ice cream in front of me and poured coffee for both of us. "I'm not going to be able to move after I eat this, you know."

"But you have to clean my carpet."

I smiled. "I'll find a way."

"I'll bet you will." We both laughed.

We finished our cobbler, freshened our coffee and went to the living room. I sat on the couch and she sat in a chair across from me.

She took a sip of coffee then set the cup on the table. "So tell me about the case you're working on and what it has to do with David Braun."

"I'm not sure yet that it has anything to do with Braun, except that he was seeing the Fouchet woman before she disappeared. Given what you told me about the other women he dated, there may be a connection."

I told her about meeting Elle in the alcove and her overwhelming desire to pee, which, at the time, was more important than meeting me. We both laughed at that. When I finished telling what we'd been able to learn so far, meager as it was, I paused, relit my pipe, and said, "After what you've told me, I'm beginning to have a bad feeling about this. There may be much more going on than we know about, and it's possible David Braun is neck deep in it. I think I'll talk to Sergeant Belden to see if he knows anything about him. Maybe that'll tell us something. Do you have an address for Braun?"

"Personnel probably does, at least they have his address at the time he quit. I didn't think to check, but will in the morning. I'll call you."

"That'll work." I smiled. "Ready to have your carpet cleaned?"

"Oh, yeah! Thought you'd never ask. I'll take the cups to the kitchen. You know where the bathroom is."

I set my pipe in the ashtray, walked down the hallway to the bathroom, and took my dopp kit from the linen closet. After washing my face and hands, brushing my teeth, and hanging my clothes, except for my shorts, on the hook on the bathroom door, I went to the bedroom.

The door was slightly ajar, and she was in bed with a pale blue sheet pulled up to just slightly over her breasts. As I slipped out of my shorts, I could smell the faint scent of her body and a light perfume.

"My God, woman, you smell delicious."

"You smell spicy. I like it."

We kissed. Gently. Then again with the passion and fire of a man and woman in love. She responded, moaning softly, as I moved downward, kissing one breast and then the other. Then I moved upward, hard and erect. She locked her legs around my body as I entered her, whispering, "Love me, Max. Love me!" Passion took us and we moved with increasing rhythm till we were lost in the intensity of the final moment.

We lay silent, out of breath, unmoving. She nibbled my ear. I could hear the smile in her voice as she said, "I'll bet I have the cleanest carpet in New York." We both laughed aloud, and a few minutes later, still smiling, fell asleep in each other's arms.

NINE

I rolled out early in the morning from Ari's. No carpet cleaning. She wanted to get to Saks early enough to talk to someone in Personnel to see if they had an address for Braun, and I wanted to get to my cave in time to shower before Pepper came in. Gotta look good for the help, you know. Also for any clients who showed up at our door.

I was sitting at my desk, finishing up a cold cup of coffee I'd picked up on the way back from Ari's, when Pepper came in just ahead of the boy from the deli with coffee and Danish. The lad set the sack on Pepper's desk, waved, and walked out. We paid our deli delivery bill once a month and always included a healthy tip for the boy.

I'd been thinking about Pepper. The raise of five dollars a week that I'd given her the previous day, though substantial during the rough economic times we were having, wasn't enough. We had a fair amount of money in the bank; cases were coming our way regularly and, in all likelihood, would continue to do so. In addition to managing the office, she also took on investigations. She had a keen, analytical mind, and one of the insurance cases we solved was because she'd been able to tie the bad guys to three other cases of fraud. I needed to do something more for her.

Pepper hung up her coat, took a coffee and Danish out of the sack, brought them into my office, and set them on my desk.

"You look spiffy this morning, boss. Smell good, too. Have a nice night?"

"I guess so," I said, smiling. "I cleaned Ari's carpet."

She looked at me for a full ten seconds. "If that means what I think it means, I ain't going to pursue it. Too early in the morning."

I just grinned.

"Yep—I was right. Eat your Danish, boss."

She was turning away when I said, "Get your coffee, come back in, and have a seat. I want to talk."

She was settled and sipping when I asked, "When did we change our office name from Grant Agency to Grant Investigations?"

She thought for a moment. "December, last year. End of December, right before Christmas. Why?"

"Why, in a minute. What are we paying you?"

"Before or after?"

"Before or after what?"

"The raise you gave me yesterday."

"After."

"Forty dollars a week."

I lit my pipe and took a couple puffs. "What are we paying me?"

"Seventy-five dollars a week."

A couple more puffs. "Hmmm ... I want to change the sign on the door and the same on our business cards."

"To what?"

"Grant and Brown Investigations, or something like that. And raise your salary to sixty-five bucks a week. I get ten more because I'm still the boss. Or at least I think I am, so humor me and call me boss."

Mouth open, she just stared. Finally, she said, "You been hitting the bourbon this morning? You can't be serious."

"But I am. You deserve it. I've been thinking about it for several weeks. You manage the office, and in addition, handle about one-third of the cases that come in. That's enough of a partnership for me."

"Boss, I could just kiss you!"

I rose slightly from my chair and looked around. "Nope."

"Nope?"

"Nope: No Bo in sight. Kiss me."

And she did, smack on the lips. Tasted good. "What lipstick is that?"

"Pink Passion."

Smiling, I said, "I envy Bo."

"I won't tell Ari."

I laughed. "Neither will I."

I set my pipe in the ashtray and took a sip of coffee. "Back to business. I have to see Jake this morning and pick up the pictures he developed for us. And speaking of Ari, she may call. It appears David Braun was involved with several women when he worked at Saks. Their Personnel department may have an address for him. If she calls with it, make a note."

"I will, Boss." Smiling, she went on, "Can I tell Ari about my promotion?"

"Sure. And maybe you two can plan an evening in the next week or so when we can get together for dinner. She'd like that, too."

I finished my Danish, hit the boys' room to wash my hands, and while drying, debated whether to carry a hand cannon. Decided not to. My smaller snubnose or even my .45 add a level of comfort when needed, or when some gut feeling tells me it's appropriate, but as comfortable as I am packing one, they're heavy.

Regis McCafferty

I slipped on my jacket and cap, put a pipe and tobacco pouch in my pocket, and with a wave at Pepper, headed out the door. My normal mode of transportation is bus or trolley, but as I stepped out the building door, a few drops of rain were hitting the sidewalk, and overhead, the sky was putty-colored and threatening. More rain on the way. I lucked out. An empty Checker cab was headed south on Flatbush and I hailed it, opened the back door, and hopped inside. It was none too soon—by the time we moved into traffic, the few drops of rain had become a torrent. I gave the cabbie Jake's address and settled back in the passenger-side corner to light my pipe and watch New York roll by in fits and starts.

We drove past the College Theater on Flatbush and I noticed that *Gunga Din*, with Cary Grant, Victor McLaglen, and Douglas Fairbanks, was playing. The College was a new theater that had just opened the previous year, and though I was pretty sure I'd enjoy *Gunga Din*, I wasn't too sure Ari would. *Love Affair*, with Charles Boyer and Irene Dunne, was more her line. Well, I could ask. One never knows. She might humor me.

I was taking gentle puffs on my pipe, my head turned toward the window, when out of the corner of my eye, I saw the cabbie glance back at me.

"That pipe smells good. Whatcha smokin' in it?"

I had to think for a couple seconds. "Ah ... Sir Walter Raleigh."

"Nice aroma. Kinda sweet and nutty. My missus, now, she can't abide cigarette or cigar smoke, but I'll bet she'd like that."

"Most drug stores carry inexpensive pipes and a fair amount of tobaccos. Wouldn't cost much to find out."

"Mebe I'll do that. What was the name of that tobacco, again?"

"Sir Walter Raleigh." I turned a bit more toward the window. Wasn't in the mood for cabbie chat. He took the hint and concentrated on peering through the sweep of the wipers at the street ahead.

Even in the rain and heavy traffic, the trip to Jake's photographic studio on Livonia took little more than twenty minutes, a trip that on bus and trolley would have taken forty. I paid the cabbie, opened the cab door, and scooted across the sidewalk to the shop. At that, I still got wet. It was pouring.

Jake was behind his desk drinking coffee, or at least drinking something from a cup. With Jake, one can never be sure.

He smiled. "Shitty weather. Want a heavy coffee?"

"Heavy?"

"Straight is light. With bourbon, it's heavy."

"Neither, actually. I just had coffee at the office and it's a might early for heavy." I paused then said, "You know, Jake, you seem to nurse that stuff all day long and I've never seen you drunk."

"Ya got it wrong, young fella. You've never seen me sober."

We both laughed as I sat down in the chair next to his desk. He reached into his desk drawer, pulled out an envelope, and handed it to me.

"I developed them last night. Wasn't sure what time you'd be here. There were twelve on the roll and seven in the camera. The ones from the roll are up front."

Of the first twelve, only one was of a person: Annette's aunt. The rest were scenes from around the neighborhood. The first one that came from the roll that had been in the camera was of a car, a 1939 Ford coupe that appeared to be medium gray. The second one simply stunned me. Mouth open, I stared then muttered, "I'll be a son of a bitch!"

Jake set his cup down. "Got a problem, Max?"

"Maybe. Don't know yet. I just slapped the hell out of this guy yesterday."

"Whatcha mean?"

So I told him about going to the local tobacconist to buy a pipe rack, and the punk that came at me like he was going to eat me up.

"Sure it was the same guy?"

"Yeah. No doubt." I looked at the photo for a few seconds. "I have a gut feeling this guy is mixed up in the disappearance of my missing woman. No proof, just a feeling."

"Your gut feelings seem to have a way of turning out right more often than not. Know where this guy lives?"

"No. At least not yet. Might have an address later today, but it'll be an old one. Could still be good, of course, but I also have a feeling like this guy moves around a bit."

I gathered up the photos and camera, promised Jake I'd get together with him for a game of chess and a drink when I had time, and left for my office.

TEN

Her name was Bertha Much, pronounced Muck. She was fat, smelly, large wart on the side of her nose, and as ugly as her name. A tough, hard bitch, Marcia thought, as she sat across the table from her in a makeshift kitchen. David had brought her here and introduced Bertha with the remark that she'd tell Marcia the rules; then he'd left.

And tell her the rules, she did. Marcia would get a room, meals, spending money, one day off a week— whatever that meant—and enough horse and coke to keep her happy. In return, Marcia would *entertain* men day or night. Longshoremen worked shifts, as did the soldiers at the Brooklyn Army Terminal.

Bertha took a sip of her coffee and looked at Marcia over the rim of the cup. "Stand up and take off your clothes ... all of them."

"Why should I—"

"You know why you're here, honey. Take off your clothes."

Marcia stood, kicked off her loafers, slipped out of her jacket and placed it on the back of her chair. Her blouse was next, and then skirt, slip, bra, and after hesitating a few seconds, her panties. She stood, naked, with her arms at her sides.

Bertha set her cup on the table. "Move away from the table and turn around."

Marcia did as she was told.

Bertha stood. "Nice bush, nice ass, firm tits. Dave sure can pick 'em. All right, honey, you can put your clothes on."

After she dressed, Marcia reached for her coffee. Her hand shook.

Bertha looked her up and down. "How you keeping?"

"Little shaky. Queasy. I got a short one from David before we left my apartment. I thought it was enough. Wasn't."

"All right. We'll fix you up, but let's get to your room first."

Martha picked up her bag, dropped it, and when she reached for it again, Bertha said, "I'll get it. Just follow me. A few of the girls work days, most work in the evening. You'll start this evening."

The brothel had originally been a small apartment building with fourteen bed-sitting rooms, all with a wash-up area. There were eight bedrooms upstairs, four on each side of a hallway, and six down, with parlor, dining room, and kitchen on the first floor. There was an additional full bath on each floor at the back end of the house.

Marcia followed her down the hallway on the first floor to the second room on the right past the parlor. Bertha opened the door and nodded her head for Marcia to go in. The room was small, but large enough for a double bed, table, and chair, and a dresser at one end. It had wood floors but several throw rugs were scattered about, one next to the bed. At one corner, curtains were drawn back to show a washbasin and toilet. A pale blue terry cloth robe hung on a hook next to the basin.

The Nude on the Postcard

Bertha set Marcia's bag down. "It's clean, and you're expected to keep it that way. There's a Hoover and cleaning items in the bath next to you. The name of the girl next door is Annette, and the one across the hall is Jean. You'll get to know the others in time. The men are pretty decent, some of them even married. We don't tolerate any rough stuff but you can get noisy if you like. The walls are thick. Some of them like screamers, but you'll figure that out quickly. And you don't take money from them. I take care of that up front. You'll find some books and magazines in the parlor, so if you want to bring some to your room it's all right.

"And something else. Important. If any of the men talk about cargo, shipping schedules, or what's going on at the Army Terminal, you're to report that to me. In fact, you should encourage it. It could mean something extra for you."

Marcia walked to the bed and sat down. "How many ..."

"It varies. Sometimes none, sometimes six in an evening. Probably four or five. If you want to do a line of coke sometime in the evening, come to the kitchen. I'll get the kit now and fix you up." As she was going out the door, she turned. "One more thing—wear only your robe after five o'clock, and douche in-between. Just plain water is best. There's new equipment for you in your wash-up area."

The room was warm, but Marcia was shivering. Streetwise as she was, she was shivering. It's all a dream, she thought, just a dream, and pretty soon I'll wake in my own apartment. But she knew it wasn't a dream, just as she knew the shivering would stop as soon as she had a fix. Then everything would be all right ... everything would be all right. Tears dropped on her lap.

ELEVEN

The first thing I noticed, as I walked down the hallway toward my office, was a guy in a white cap and coveralls, the stub of an unlit cigar in his mouth. He was sitting on a tall stool, scraping my name off the glass in the door. He glanced at me when I stopped. "Gimme ten seconds."

I nodded. And that's all it took. The "t" from "Grant" disappeared. He scooted out of the way and I went in. Pepper was reading the front page of the city edition of the *New York Times*, so I stopped at her desk and read a couple of the column headlines upside down: *OUTNUMBERED R.A.F. CLAIMS THREE VICTORIES; NORWEGIANS FACE DEMAND BY REICH; LA GUARDIA YIELDS IN UNION DISPUTE OVER SUBWAY PACT.*

She glanced up. "You want the puzzles page?"

"Nope. We have puzzles enough." I nodded at the newspaper. "Anything new in there?"

"Same book, different page."

I put my coat and hat on the rack. "I saw the sign painter on the way in. What's it going to read?"

"'Grant and Brown Associates,' with an ampersand between 'Grant' and 'Brown.' 'Private Investigations' below. Same on the business cards. Our phone number on the right bottom, and our full names will appear at the bottom left of the card, yours on top."

I smiled. "As it should be. I like being on top."

She smiled back. "I ain't goin' there, boss."

"Pour me a coffee, grab yours, and come into my cave. I have a story to tell, and a photo to show you."

When she was settled in the side chair next to my desk, I told her about my trip to the local tobacconist to get a rack, and the guy who slammed into me. The guy who was going to clean my clock, till I slapped him. I pulled a photo out of the pack Jake had processed. "That's the guy. That's David Braun."

"Well, I'll be damned."

"Yeah, I said something similar to Jake, but a bit more colorful."

"You know where this guy lives?"

"No. Ari hasn't called, has she? She said she'd check the Personnel record for his last address and phone us."

"No, not yet. What's your feeling about this? Other than the dating connection, we don't have anything that connects Braun to Annette's disappearance."

"I swear, Pepper, I really don't know. According to Ari, rumors at Saks circulated about him getting a couple women hooked on drugs, and they've either quit, or simply quit showing up. No one has seen them since. Same with Annette, except she'd already left Saks before she disappeared. And you would think Elle is streetwise enough to know if her own daughter were using drugs."

"Maybe not if it was early days for Annette. It's pretty easy to cover up using when you just start. No track marks, no runny nose or watering eyes. Of course, if she'd just had a fix, she'd look and sound all right as well."

"I think you know more about it than I do"

"When I was in college, I had a couple friends who did the jazz scene in Harlem. They both used cocaine. I don't know if they were addicted, but they used it regularly. I don't have any firsthand experience. It scared the hell out of me."

"I tried weed a couple times a few years back when I was working construction in Chicago, but that's the extent of my drug experience. Bourbon is better."

She stood and picked up her cup. "Ya know, there's something weird about this whole setup. Let's say Braun got them hooked. Why? The main reason might be that he's using and needs customers to support his own habit. That's common. Makes sense. What doesn't make sense is why they'd disappear. If he's hooked, he needs them as income to support his own habit."

"Yeah ... Now I know why I made you a partner. I'm going to give Sergeant Belden a call. Even if he doesn't know anything about Braun, he might have some other ideas."

I took my address book from my top desk drawer, looked up the number of the 68th Precinct station, and dialed. It was picked up on the third ring.

"68th Precinct, Adams."

"Is Sergeant Belden in?"

"Who's calling?"

"Max Grant."

"Oh—Grant. He is and he ain't."

"That tells me a helluva lot, Ron." I knew Ron Adams from several years before, when I was a cop. He was close to retirement so they took him off the streets and gave him a desk job. Good thing. He was slow and fat and mooched handouts from just about every restaurant on his beat. Aside from that, he was a prick.

Ron cleared his throat. "He's out back in the stables."

"Jesus! They got him on horse patrol?"

"Nah ... He's having a serious discussion with one of his snitches. Want me to get him?"

"No. Just tell him to call me from the station, or when he gets home. He has my number."

"Will do. You take it easy, Grant."

"Yeah. You, too."

The 68th Precinct station was located at the corner of Fourth Avenue and Forty-third Street in Brooklyn, with horse stables at the rear of the building. Access to the stables from the station was through a brick walkway. I didn't know who designed the stationhouse, but it always reminded me of pictures I'd seen of small Scottish castles. It had a round turret structure at the right-front corner that looked like it could house a cannon. For all I knew, it did.

If Belden had taken a snitch to the stables for a *serious discussion,* it was so no one in the station would hear the smacks, grunts, and groans as he got his point across. And it was strange Adams was so nice to me. Not his usual demeanor. Maybe it was because I asked for Belden—hell, who knows?

I had just finished cleaning the dottle from my pipe and refilling it with Edgeworth, when the phone rang. Pepper picked it up and I heard her say, "Yeah, hold on a sec, Ari."

I picked up my phone. "How's the love of my life this afternoon?"

"Harried, harassed, and ready to be hugged."

I laughed. "Can't do anything about the first two. I take it you're not in a crowd."

"I'm in the Personnel director's office. She stepped out for a cup of coffee. Braun's record here was decent. He only missed two days' work in eleven months—I thought he'd missed more—but when he left, it was without notice, and we have twelve dollars on the books that we still owe him. We sent a letter to his last known address, but it was returned as 'moved with no forwarding address.' Actually, he had two addresses, but one was crossed off. Do you want them both?"

"Yeah, I'd better." I wrote them down and noticed one of them was near Sergeant Belden's Sixty-eighth Precinct Station. I asked which one was lined out.

"The address on Thirty-ninth Street, is just off Fourth Avenue from the looks of the number."

"Is there anything in his file that would indicate he was doing drugs?"

"No, nothing. Like I said, he only missed two days' work the whole time he was here. There were those rumors that he dealt drugs to some of the women here, but nothing solid to go on." She paused a few seconds. "Will you be coming over to my place this evening?"

"I don't think so, honey. I'm going to do some nosing around—maybe check out Braun's old addresses and the neighborhood."

"Probably just as well. I'll miss you next to me, but I have to be in here early tomorrow morning. Be careful."

"I will. Bye, honey."

I looked at the addresses then pulled a city map from my desk drawer. The most current address Saks had was on Fifty-third Street—near Third Avenue, if my memory hadn't deserted me. Both were in the Sunset Park area, though the crossed-out address on Thirty-ninth Street was right at the northern boundary near Green Wood cemetery, the current residence of our one-time mayor, Boss Tweed, albeit six feet under. Green Wood was considered the proper burial place for Christian Protestants of good reputation, and one of the early rules was that no one executed for a crime or even someone who died in jail could be buried there. But Tweed, who died in Ludlow Street Jail, managed to get around the rule, just as he had gotten around the rules in life.

For a few seconds, I debated packing a gun. Prudence won out. I was going into an area not known for good cheer and happy nightlife, and it would undoubtedly be nighttime before I made it to the second address. I thought it unlikely I'd run into Braun, or any other troublemaker, but strange things seem to happen to me after the sun goes down. Aside from that, I wanted to try out a new holster I'd bought for my snubnose.

Standard shoulder holsters are convenient but, in my opinion, also bulky and sloppy. The straps that cross on my back just below my shirt collar bother me. And the tie-down strap that hooks to my belt is never snug enough, so that sometimes, depending on my movement, the holster flaps back and forth. It also tends to slant away from my body when sitting. The new holster is actually a left-hand holster with belt slots so that it can be carried on the left side. If I turned it around, however, so the slots were on the outside, and ran my belt through the slots on my left side, the holster fit snugly between my belt and pants, tight up against my body and fine for a right-hand draw across my body.

I was in the process of taking my belt off when Pepper walked in and stopped just inside the doorway. "If you're going any further with that bump-and-grind routine, boss, I'm going for a walk."

I laughed, held up the holster, finished putting it on, then went to the floor safe for my .38. We keep our handguns in the safe unless there's some reason to carry or have one in a desk drawer. "Both addresses Ari gave me are in the Sunset Park area, so I'm headed there to wander around a bit. See what I can dig up on Braun. Both addresses are old, according to Ari, but I might be able to get a lead from someone. Just lock up about five. Tell Bo I said hi. Oh, if Sergeant Belden calls, tell him I'll call him later this evening when I get back."

On a hunch I might need it, I took one of the pictures of Annette from my desk drawer and put it in my shirt pocket. I put my coat and hat on, slipped my pipe and tobacco pouch in my pocket, waved, and went out the door. Didn't even think about a bus or trolley. I wanted to get to the Thirty-ninth Street address while it was still light, so I flagged a cab.

TWELVE

I had the cab drop me at Fourth Avenue and Thirty-ninth Street and walked west on Thirty-ninth. It was a bit farther from Green Wood cemetery than I originally thought by about four blocks. The north side of the street held some small shops and what appeared to be a few vacant buildings. The address Ari had given me was on the south side of the street in an old but well-kept apartment building. The bottom button at the door was marked *Manager*, but I didn't see Braun's name next to the buzzers above it, so I rang the manager's buzzer and waited. I was about to ring it again when the door opened and I was confronted with a middle-aged Teutonic Amazon. She was damn near six feet tall, frizzy blonde with dark roots, blue eyes, and a nose that looked like it had been broken at one time.

"Yeah—vhadaya vant?"

It never ceases to amaze me how fast the mind works. Being myself wasn't going to get me anywhere with Brunhilde, but perhaps a German name would. "My name is Jakob Kohl and I worked with David Braun. I haven't seen him for a while, but he gave me this address several months ago. Does he still live here?"

"No!" She started to close the door.

"I owe him money. Do you know where he moved to?"

That stopped the door. "*Wie viel* ... How much?"

It had to be enough, and ten wasn't going to get it. "Twenty dollars." I could see the wheels turning.

"You giff to me, I giff to him"

"I'd rather give it to him myself. Do you know where he lives?"

"*Er schuldet mir Geld* ... Hmmm ... He owes me money."

"How much?"

"Ten dollars."

She may have recently got off the boat, but she wasn't stupid. "If I give you the ten dollars he owes you, will you answer some questions?"

She nodded.

I got my wallet out and fingered a ten. "Why did he leave here?"

"*Viele fraulein* ... Many women. Young women. I trow him out."

"How many women?"

She shrugged "Twenty?"

"What else?"

"Trinking. Maybe trugs. Bad women."

"How long did he live here?"

"Four months."

"Where did he move to?"

"*Vielleicht, dreiundfunfzig* ... Maybe Fifty-third street. Near docks."

I handed her the ten, thanked her, and headed back to Fourth Avenue to pick up a taxi. On a warm summer day with time to kill, I might have walked the twelve blocks or so to Fifty-third Street, but it was getting chilly and I was feeling lazy. I was ten minutes standing on the corner of Fourth and Thirty-ninth before I was able to catch a taxi headed south. I told the driver Fifty-third and Third Avenue, fished my pipe and pouch from my pocket, filled and lit it.

I hadn't gotten much from the apartment manager except confirmation of some things about Braun we already knew. The exception was the "many women" comment. Twenty women were a bunch, and it may have been more if Brunhilde had missed some. I suspect she had. I hadn't asked the apartment manager's name, and I'm not sure where I came up with the moniker Brunhilde, but it seemed to fit.

I paid the cabbie and walked west on Fifty-third Street toward the docks. It was an old neighborhood, a shabby neighborhood, with a few storefronts scattered among older brick houses and a few apartment buildings. I found the one I was looking for, and while not inviting in any sense, it was in much better condition than the surrounding buildings. It was composed of eight apartments in two sections of four each, two down and two up. There was an entrance at each end of the building for each group of four apartments. I went into the first entrance I came to. There were four mailboxes, one marked *Manager*, with a buzzer underneath. I buzzed then looked around. To my right, one flight of stairs went down to what must be the basement. One flight up, I could see a door on either side of the landing and the stairs went up from there to what I assumed were the upstairs apartments.

The door on the left side of the landing opened, and a short, wiry, middle-aged man stepped out. He looked like a tough old bird, with salt-and-pepper hair, and a heavy mustache to match.

"We don't have any vacant apartments."

I decided to use the same line as I did with Brunhilde. "My name is Jakob Kohl, and I worked with David Braun. I haven't seen him for a while, and I've forgotten the exact apartment number that he gave me. Does he still live here?"

"No." He started to go back inside.

"Do you know where he moved to? I owe him ten bucks and would like to pay him." I wasn't going to spring for another twenty if I could help it.

He paused and turned toward me. "He'll never miss ten dollars."

"Why do you say that?"

"He always had money when he lived here—a lot of it. New car, flashy clothes, women, all new furniture when he moved in. And I had the impression he had another apartment somewhere at the same time he had this one."

"What gave you that impression?" I was on a roll with this guy.

"I overheard some remarks made by some of the women he brought here."

I fished Annette's photo out of my shirt pocket, walked up the steps, and showed it to him. "This wouldn't happen to be one of the women, would it?"

He took the photo, looked, pushed his glasses down on his nose, and held it at arm's length. "Yeah ... could be. Yeah ... I think so. She came here several times with him."

"When did you last see her?"

"Several weeks ago, just before he moved out."

You mean Braun lived here till a few weeks ago?" If true, that meant Braun had the apartment on Thirty-ninth at the same time he had this one.

"Yeah. Days. He moved about ten days ago."

"You know where he moved to?"

"Not exactly, but one of the movers said they were going to Bay Ridge ... Sixty-eighth Street, maybe. Near the Shore Road, at any rate." He handed the photo back and peered at me over his glasses. "You don't owe him ten bucks, do you?"

"No."

"You owe me ten bucks."

"Yes." I pulled out my wallet and handed the guy a ten.

He smiled, and without another look at me, went into his apartment and closed the door. I walked out of the building, stopped on the sidewalk, lit my pipe, and walked slowly back toward Third Avenue, thinking.

The first thing that came to mind was a question. If Braun had the kind of money he seemed to have, what the hell had he been doing working stock at Saks? More questions: What was the source of his money? Why rent more than one apartment, even if he had the money? What about the women, particularly the ones who have disappeared? And given my flair for cockeyed instinct, perhaps the most intriguing question: why are all the apartments near the docks?

Sherlock Holmes would undoubtedly call this a three-pipe problem. I'd settle for one pipe and a tall bourbon, so I flagged a taxi and headed back to my cave, hoping I could get hold of Sergeant Beldon. Any information would be welcome.

After hitting my stash cabinet for a glass and couple ounces of bourbon and my bedroom for some ice from my small refrigerator, I parked my butt at my desk. There were two notes from Pepper. The first was that Belden had phoned saying he'd be home about seven o'clock. I looked at my watch. Seven twenty. The second note was that Elle phoned wanting to know if we had learned anything. Pepper wrote that she told her we were following some leads, and that I was out of the office now, doing just that. She also added that Elle sounded sober.

I called Belden. He picked up on the second ring.

"Belden."

"Grant. What's this I hear about you talking to horses this afternoon?"

"You'd be amazed at how many of those nags talk back."

"Get anything good?"

"A promise. He'll keep it or I'll shove a bag of oats up his ass."

I laughed. "I need some information."

"I figured. Like what?"

"I'm chasing another missing woman. Young woman of twenty-two named Annette Fouchet. More important is the guy who may be responsible, a David Braun. Twenty-eight to thirty years old, five feet eight or nine, maybe 140 pounds. Brown hair. Clean-shaven. Pushy attitude. Lives, and maybe works, near the docks between the Army Terminal and Red Hook."

"Brown?"

"Yeah, but spelled B-R-A-U-N. German."

"Sounds like you've seen him."

"Yeah, you could say that. I'll tell you about it over a beer sometime soon."

"The name is familiar. Seems we talked to him about some missing women a while back. I'll have to look up my notes and refresh my memory."

"If I'm not here and it's during the day, leave any information with Pepper."

"You know, Grant, you should give that lady a raise. You couldn't run your office without her."

"I did. Made her a partner."

"Well, I'll be damned. You're smarter than I thought."

I smiled. "Sometimes. Call if you remember anything. And thanks."

I sat back in my chair, took a sip of whiskey, and lit my pipe. After a couple moments, I picked up the phone and dialed Elle's boarding house. I let it ring about ten times and was ready to hang up when a familiar voice answered.

"Hello?"

"That you, Elle?"

"Mr. Grant?"

"Yep. And call me Max. I'm spending your money." We hadn't cashed in her stone yet, but she didn't know that.

"Have you found out anything about Annette?"

She did sound sober. I was surprised. "Not directly, but I think there may be some connection with her boyfriend, David Braun. I'm following up on that by trying to locate him. No luck so far, but I visited the last two places he lived and have a lead on the area he may be living in now. I also know a cop who will do some checking for me. I know it doesn't sound like much, but it's a good start."

"It sounds like you've been busy. Thank you." She paused. Then she asked, "Is there anything I can do to help?"

"Not at the moment. No ... I take that back. Maybe there is. Tomorrow, would you go to the Bowery Mission and see if you can find Jake? If he isn't there, leave a message with one of the group leaders or supervisors asking him to come to my office."

"If he's there, he may ask why."

"Just tell him I may need some help locating someone. You can tell him more if you like, but I think I'd hold off doing that for now. It's up to you, though."

"I'll just tell him you need him. Anything else?"

"I may need you for the same thing. You and Jake together. It could involve a lot of walking."

"I can do that." I heard a smile in her voice and thought, *I'll bet you can.* I didn't follow up with a comment.

"Don't stray too far from the house. If you're going to leave for more than a couple hours during the day, call us and let us know."

"All right, Max. I'll call tomorrow after I go to the Mission, whether I see Jake or not."

"That'll be fine, Elle ... And listen—we'll find your daughter."

"Thank you. I needed to hear that."

"Good night, Elle."

I set the phone on its cradle and stared at it for a moment before I picked up my pipe and lit it. I took short puffs, still staring at the phone, and hoping I hadn't lied to Elle. I had a bad feeling about this case. It was nebulous, and though we'd collected scattered bits and pieces of information, we had no common thread to tie them together. No common thread unless it was David Braun, and I had some suspicions about that twerp, whether he was involved with Annette's disappearance or not. The guy obviously had money from some source, so again, what was he doing taking a job at Saks as a stock clerk for twenty bucks a week or less? And the girls he dates while there either disappear or quit. Then he quits.

The exception was Annette, who went to another job, but then disappeared in short order. Another job ... What was it Elle said? Annette had taken a position as a French translator for some scientists at the physics lab at Columbia University. That was in January. She disappeared about the middle of March.

I reached for the phone and dialed Elle's number again. It was picked up on the eighth ring. A man's voice.

"Hello?"

"Hello. I'm calling for Elle Fouchet. Is she in?"

"Wait a minute. I'll see." It was less than a minute.

"Hello?"

"Hello Elle, it's Max again. Who was the guy that answered the phone?"

"Mr. White. Harold White. He owns the house. Why?"

"Just curious. An old detective habit. I have a question—actually, two questions. You said Annette was hired as a translator at Columbia. Who did she work for, and is translation all she did?"

"Let me think ... She also kept track of correspondence from other scientists, filing, mostly. The only person I remember her mentioning is a Professor Dunning, but I don't know if she worked directly for him or not."

"Thanks, Elle. At least that's a starting point."

"Are you going to talk with them?"

"I think it would be wise. They may or may not have any useful information, but we can't overlook the possibility. I'll let you know if we hear anything helpful. Thanks again."

It was early enough, and I thought about phoning Ari, but nixed the idea. If I talked with her, I'd want to go to her place, and I'd had enough running around for the day. Instead, I decided to go to the deli a half block away for a sandwich and Coke, then get to bed at a decent hour. I also decided to talk with Pepper about going to see the people at Columbia, or at least calling them. Some background on Professor Dunning might be helpful, and Pepper was good at such things. Maybe it would be smart for both of us to visit the school. I grabbed my coat, hat, stuffed my pipe in my pocket, and headed out the door.

Regis McCafferty

THIRTEEN

She'd been soaking in the tub, head just above water, for about ten minutes, in water as hot as she could stand it. She sat up, got to her knees, picked up the bar of Lifebuoy soap, and thoroughly soaped a white washcloth to a pale, coral-colored froth. Face, neck, underarms, breasts, stomach—she dreaded the thought of touching herself between her legs but did anyway. Gently. She grimaced, moaned. She held the washcloth there for a moment then slid back down in the tub.

She was ragged. Edgy. Her last heroin fix had been about two in the morning, just after ... just after ... "Oh, God," she cried, "how did this happen to me?"

There was a tap at the bathroom door. "You all right in there?"

"Yeah," she said quietly. "All right ... I'll be out in a couple minutes."

"Take your time. I peed before I left my room."

She knelt again, pulled the plug, stood, and picked up the towel that was lying folded on the small cabinet next to the tub. She dried, slipped on panties then robe, and opened the door.

Marcia, wrapped in a pale blue terry robe, was leaning against the wall smoking a cigarette. She stepped forward and held out her hand.

"My name's Marcia. I think you're the girl next door to me."

"Annette. My name is Annette." She leaned forward to take Marcia's hand but almost fell, and would have if Marcia hadn't put her hand to Annette's shoulder.

"Whoa, girl, you look beat. Better sit for a minute." Marcia led her back into the bathroom, tossed her cigarette in the toilet, put the lid down, and patted the lid, saying, "Sit here," as she sat on the edge of the tub.

"How long have you been here, Annette?"

"Two weeks ... three weeks ... not sure. Maybe more, maybe less. I've lost track." Her head was down as if staring at her slippers, her long hair falling forward covering both sides of her face. She shivered.

Marcia reached out, put her hand under Annette's chin and raised her head. Tears were streaming down her face.

Frowning, Marcia asked, "How old are you, kid?"

"Twenty-two."

"Jesus! Braun get you hooked?"

Annette nodded.

"Promised you an endless supply of horse and coke?"

Annette nodded again.

"And all you had to do was live here and make a few men happy from time to time, huh?"

Annette wiped her eyes with her sleeve. "I burn so bad ... Just raw." She pointed to herself below her waist. "Too many ... too often."

"You tell Bertha?"

She shook her head. "No. I'm afraid."

Marcia reached in her robe pocket for her cigarettes, flipped one from the pack to her hand, and lit it. "Afraid of Bertha?"

"Maybe. Maybe David." She paused. Then she looked directly at Marcia. "There was a girl who complained a lot. At least, that's what I was told. Her name was Nancy and she disappeared a few days after I came here. I didn't ask Bertha about her, but one of the other girls said she was here on a Saturday night— gone on Sunday morning. No one knew where. No one asked, either. David sometimes comes here late on Saturday nights ..."

Marcia inhaled deeply, blew smoke toward the ceiling, then took Annette by the arm and stood her up. "Come on, let's go see Bertha. She may have some cream or something that will ease the burning. And maybe something to take the edge off. You look like you could use it."

They found Bertha sitting in the kitchen, having a cup of coffee. She smiled. "I see you two neighbors have met."

Marcia pulled out a chair and motioned Annette to sit down. She wasn't smiling. "Yeah, we've met. Aside from needing a short fix, Annette has another problem. A painful, raw, burning problem."

Bertha set her cup down. "Clap?"

"More like overuse and maybe some rough sex. She needs some medication and a couple days off."

"She has a day off coming in two days."

"Then give her the next two days off plus the one she has scheduled. Let her rest up a bit. Give her something for the pain and some horse."

Bertha, angry, stood and took her coffee cup to the sink. "Who's running this place, goddamn it, me or you?"

"Neither of us. David Braun is ... Look, Bertha, use some common sense. If Annette is moaning in pain and not in supposed ecstasy, the guys will know it. That hurts business, and Braun will be pissed. We both know some of the guys have favorites. Do any of them ask for her?"

Bertha thought for a few seconds. "Yeah, a couple."

"All right, then. Just tell Braun you're protecting his investment. I know David. That'll make sense to him."

Bertha went to the small safe in the corner next to the refrigerator, opened it, and took out the kit for a fix. "Where do you want it?"

Annette pulled up her robe and turned her right leg. "Back of my knee."

After giving her the shot, Bertha opened a drawer at the counter and took out a small jar of cannabis cream and handed it to Annette with the comment that it should soothe any raw or painful area.

Marcia looked at the label. "I thought that stuff was banned a few years ago."

Bertha shrugged. "It was." She didn't elaborate. "Wash each time before you put it on, maybe every six hours or so. You have three days to get well. Make sure you do."

When they got back to their rooms, Annette stopped, turned, and put her arms around Marcia, hugged, and then moved back toward her door. "Thank you for stepping in and helping me. I'd have never been able to do that on my own ... I don't have the courage. And I feel better now, after the fix. When I feel better, I want to get out, get away from this—this hell." She was close to tears again. "But then it wears off, and I know there's no place to go, no place warm and safe, no place to hide."

"Do you have any family?"

"I lived with my aunt, but she'd never accept me back in her house if she knew about this."

Marcia smiled. "Lie. Anyone else?"

"My mother. I think she'd understand because she's had a rough life at times. Still does. Lots of ups and downs, mostly downs lately. Much of her life was spent in France, but she's been back in New York for a while. Funny—it just occurred to me that I don't know where she lives."

"Father?"

"Never knew him." It was Annette's turn to smile. "Not sure my mother did. She was a model in Paris for some years. She's in her forties but still looks good—looks much younger."

"On the streets?"

"Maybe. I don't know. Never asked. It isn't something a girl would ask her mother, is it?"

"No, I guess not ..." Marcia shrugged. "You ever mess with drugs before David?"

"No, never. Never even smoked cigarettes."

"Sex?"

Annette blushed. "No."

"David?"

"Yes."

"You know, Annette, you need to get off horse and coke and find your way back to your old world. You'll die here if you don't."

"What about you?"

A petulant smile quickly crossed Marcia's face and then was gone. "Me? I've pretty much run out of options and hope. You're young. You have a chance."

Annette leaned against the edge of her doorway. "I don't think we can just get out of here. I haven't asked and I haven't tried. From what little I've seen, the back door is barred, the windows are barred, and Bertha controls the front door. If we need something, we make a list and give it to her. Our things are delivered the next day, but I don't know how."

Marcia paused a few seconds. "Well, best you get into your room and use that salve. If you feel better later, tap on my door and we'll have some lunch. In the meantime, I'll think about breaking you out of this place." She started to turn away but turned back. "I swear, if I had a gun, I'd kill David Braun, even if it meant the electric chair!"

The look on her face told Annette she meant it.

FOURTEEN

As I moved through my morning routine of toilet, shower, and shave, I kept thinking of what I'd told Elle the night before—that we'd find her daughter. But it had been more than two weeks since she'd gone missing, and if we did find her, it was just as likely we'd find her dead as alive. And at the stumblebum rate we were going, if we did find her, it would probably be by accident.

After I finished dressing, I walked through my office, through Pepper's cave to the front door, unlocked and opened it. Our morning cups of coffee and two Danish were sitting outside the door as usual. Sometimes the kid who delivers makes it before Pepper gets in and sometimes not. This morning, he was a few minutes early. We had an office coffee maker and Pepper usually made a pot midmorning, but for some reason, the coffee that came from the deli always tasted better.

I had just settled at my desk with coffee and Danish when Pepper came in, hung up her coat and headscarf, and went to her desk.

After a sip of coffee, I said, "Hey, Pepper, grab your coffee and Danish and come in here. We need to talk about this case for a bit."

As she sat down next to my desk, I could smell the faint aroma of lavender. "You and Bo share a bubble bath this morning?"

"Uh-huh, I bathed and he bubbled."

I took a few seconds trying to wrap my mind around that. Couldn't. "I'm not going there."

"Yeah, best you don't. The explanation could get complicated."

Not sure whether to make a poor attempt at a reply or take a sip of coffee, I chose the easy way out, sipped coffee, set the cup down, and filled her in on what information I'd gathered on Braun the night before.

"I went to sleep last night—alone, I might add—thinking about this damned case. I talked with Elle late last evening and told her we'd find her daughter." Pepper raised an eyebrow. "Yeah, I know ... but she was sober, concerned, and trying to be helpful. I had to tell her something. I also talked with Belden. He's going to check around to see if he can come up with something on David Braun. He didn't really know the name, so I don't have a lot of hope there. I did ask Elle who Annette worked for at the university, and she told me the only name that had been mentioned was a Professor Dunning. It might be worth seeing him, if we can, to ask a few questions. What do you think? In fact, what do you think of this whole mess?"

"You want my opinion based on what we have so far, or intuition—what you call gut feeling?"

"Let's go with gut feeling. I know what we have so far. Squat."

"All right. Then let's go with what we don't have."

"What do you mean?"

"We have no indication she's just run off, or at least there doesn't appear to be any reason for her to do that. We have no reason to think she was kidnapped, or at least kidnapped for the usual reasons. There's been no ransom note, and besides, there's no money in that family, even with Elle's stones. We can assume she wasn't unhappy with her job because that sort of thing would be important enough that Elle would have mentioned it, but we can confirm that next time we talk with her. So let's rule all that out."

I picked up my pipe. "Where's that leave us?"

"Drugs."

"Huh?"

"Drugs—like I said yesterday—drugs. That's the one single thread that runs all through this case. If Braun got her hooked, I mean bad hooked, she'd be ashamed to tell her mother or anyone else."

"Drugs cost money."

"If you're a woman, what's the one thing you got to sell?"

"Yeah, I know, I know. I just don't like to think it. Prostitution is pretty much rampant in some parts of the city, Brownsville in particular, but a lot of them are immigrants, some with pimps and some without. And the image I have of Annette is that she's lived a pretty sheltered life in spite of her mother. If you met her aunt, you'd know what I mean. Braun may have been the first man in her life. And it's a giant leap from there, to hooking on the streets."

"I wasn't thinking of something like Rosie Gold and her Midnight Rose Candy Store."

The candy store was on the corner of Saratoga and Livonia Avenues in Brownsville, Brooklyn. Rosie Gold was the seemingly innocuous elderly woman who owned the store, but it was the center of a large and well-known prostitution ring. More than that, it was the not-so-secret headquarters of one of the most infamous and deadly groups in the history of organized crime: Murder Incorporated, a death squad composed of mostly Jewish and Italian gangsters.

I lit my pipe. Thinking time. "I can't even imagine a connection between Gold and Annette. But maybe, if she's hooked, she's not on the streets. Maybe Braun is running a house. Maybe all his working girls are druggies."

She took a sip of coffee. "That's the line I think we should follow. From what you learned yesterday, Braun seems to favor the dock area. If he's running a brothel, that's probably where it's at."

"And his customers are probably longshoremen and military."

"That'd be my guess."

"We could use someone who really knows that area. Bo works—"

"No, boss. I don't want Bo involved. Look ... Bo is negro. It took him a long time to get on as a longshoreman, and the reason he's still working is because damn few can keep up with him. He works hard, keeps his mouth shut, and minds his own business. No."

"I'm sorry, Pepper. I mean that. I wasn't thinking. We do have a couple guys who might help—that is, if I can get hold of them. Remember Jake who helped us out in December on the Sarah Bennett case? I asked Elle if she saw him at the Mission to have him stop by our office. At the time, I didn't have a job for him. Just had a feeling we might need him. And there's always Murphy. He helped us out in December as well, and he's retired now."

Murphy was an old Irish cop I knew from years ago during my short stint as a member of the NYPD. Hell, everyone knew Murphy. He'd been a beat cop his entire career and trained more rookies than anyone on the entire force. If he had a first name, no one knew it. He was simply known as Murphy or Murph. When he had a year left before retirement, they pulled him in and gave him a desk job. They thought they were doing him a favor, but he hated it. They gave him a silver watch, turned him out, and so far as I knew, the only beat he patrolled now was walking his dog in his neighborhood.

My short-lived adventure with New York's finest ended with a mistake after less than two years. My mistake was in thinking the courts were too slow in dispensing justice in certain circumstances, and I appointed myself to that esteemed office. There were situations when precinct captains looked the other way, and occasionally, I took advantage of it. I was a beat cop on the Lower East Side, working the night shift, when a young woman came running out of a tenement screaming that her boyfriend was beating their three-month-old baby. I stormed into the room just as he was raising his hand over the child who was in a crib, screaming and crying. He stopped, put both his hands up and said, "Whoa." I took it to mean he was resisting arrest. That's what I told the sergeant, anyway. The ambulance attendant said he had broken ribs, broken nose, his right ear hanging on by a thread and various other contusions and lacerations. Those wooden tire thumpers we carried were deadly.

That one was overlooked. The one that got me in real trouble was when I stepped in between a man and his wife who were fighting outside a nightclub. Well, he was throwing punches and she was the punching bag. I watched while he hit her twice with his fist. She went down the second time. When she got up, he raised his fist for a third time. I grabbed his arm, spun him around, and told him to try me. He did. He swung, I took a half step back, then laid my stick on his head right above his left ear. He went down in a heap, out cold. His mistake and mine—his because he took a swing at me; mine because I laid him out. His brother was a ward captain and I got ten days off without pay. Politics. But by the time the ten days were up, I had a job collecting bad accounts for a bank, and there were a lot of them in 1935. Lousy job, but for over a year, it paid the bills.

Pepper stood up. "I think I'll put a pot of coffee on ... Just a thought, but maybe a woman could pick up some useful information in the dock area."

"I was thinking the same thing. Elle?"

"Yeah, Elle. She's streetwise and unlikely to get into any trouble she couldn't handle."

"I'll talk with her. See what she thinks. But if I do that, I'll have to tell her what we suspect. Not sure how that will go over."

"Probably piss her off, but she's been around. Knows the score."

Pepper was headed out of my office when the phone rang. I picked it up. "Grant and Brown Investigations."

"Belden. Is this Grant or Brown?" I could hear the smile in his voice.

"Screw you."

"That's been done before—in more ways than you'd care to know."

"I'll let that pass. Find out anything?"

"Yes and no."

"Oh, that's cryptic. If one of your snitches gave you that kind of answer, you'd have him talking to the horses in your backyard."

"You remember an assistant DA, back when you wore blue, named Tom Sawyer?"

"Yeah, and he was actually from Missouri where Mark Twain's novel took place. I never had any dealings with him, but heard he was a decent enough fellow."

I heard Belden sneeze. "Damned weather! I think I'm getting a cold. At any rate, Sawyer isn't with the department anymore. He's an FBI agent. I think you need to talk with him."

"About Braun?"

"Yeah, about Braun. He's running a cathouse, or at least backing one. Some of his ladies in waiting went missing and we asked a few questions but got nowhere. Sergeant Malone of the harbor patrol told me he thought the FBI was interested in the area brothels, and they also had an interest in Braun. Unless you know someone else in the Bureau, you might want to look up Sawyer. Depending on what their interest is in Braun, you might get some useful information. Then again, those FBI guys can be pretty closed mouth about any active investigations."

"I appreciate this, Belden. I really do. Thanks. I owe you."

"I like it when somebody owes me. I won't forget."

Smiling, I replied, "I'm sure you won't, and won't let me forget either."

I opened my desk drawer, took out the phone directory and looked up "Federal" anything. Found it. The FBI field office was located in the Federal Courts Building on Foley Square. I thought for a moment about how to approach the FBI and then dialed. It rang once.

"Federal Bureau of Investigation, Agent Owens speaking."

"Mr. Owens, my name is Max Grant, former NYPD policeman. I'd like to speak with one of your agents, Thomas Sawyer."

One moment, please."

A click, no other sound, then, "Sawyer speaking."

"Mr. Sawyer, my name is Max Grant. I'm no longer a police officer, but was during the time you were with the DA's office. I'm currently a private investigator working on a case that you might have an interest in, but I need some information."

"Mr. Grant, we generally cooperate with police departments, but it's not our policy to share information with private agencies."

I could sense he was ready to hang up. "All right, I understand, but does the name David Braun mean anything to you?"

Long pause. "What do you know about David Braun?"

"Damned little, but maybe more than you do."

"Do you drink coffee, Mr. Grant?"

"All day long."

"Where are you located?"

"Brooklyn. Flatbush Avenue."

"You familiar with Tom's restaurant on Washington?"

"Yeah, just south of Sterling Place."

"What do you look like?"

"Just shy of six feet, 175 pounds or so, dark mustache."

"11:30?"

"That will be fine."

"See you then." Click.

I picked up my pipe and tamped and relit it while thinking Sawyer was a bit more abrupt than I remembered him being while an assistant DA. Then again, I didn't know him that well when I was a cop. One thing for sure: *David Braun* was a magic name.

I stood, stretched, and walked out to Pepper's domain. "Why would the FBI have an unusually keen interest in David Braun?"

She looked up from the newspaper she was reading. "The FBI? You can bet it ain't because he's running a brothel, if that's what he's doing. Who called?"

"That was Belden. He pointed me to an ex–assistant DA named Tom Sawyer who is now with the FBI. I called Sawyer, told him we had an interest in Braun, and he invited me for coffee at 11:30."

"The FBI tends to leave local stuff to local cops, so it has to be more than that. We could be moving into deep doo-doo, boss."

"Maybe. But we've taken on a case to find a missing girl, and I'm not going to back away from that."

"Can I make a suggestion?"

"Sure."

"Don't tell the FBI you're going to continue come hell or high water, Max. Sometimes the most intelligent *something* you can say is *nothing*."

"That's a neat saying. Where'd you hear that?"

"Bo."

"He's a sharp guy. How did you meet him, anyway?"

"At a bar in Harlem. He smelled my perfume and followed me into the women's restroom and right into the stall. Small stall—big hands."

"Jesus! I'm not going there, either."

"Smart."

Tom's in Prospect Heights had opened in 1936 as a family restaurant and was family owned. It had a reputation for good food, decent prices, and friendly atmosphere. The walls were lined with all types of bric-a-brac, including plates, flowers—some real, some not—in wall-mounted vases, a stained glass window that looked out on nothing, and a great soda fountain. It seemed cluttered with tables and booths but was so neatly laid out that there was plenty of room. I took a booth about two-thirds of the way down one wall from the door where I could watch people coming and going. Sawyer came in five minutes later, spotted me before I could raise my hand, walked to the booth and slid in. He was as I remembered him, medium height and weight, sandy-colored hair and brown eyes, but he'd shaved the mustache he'd sported while with the DA's office.

He smiled. "Now that I see you, I remember you. You nabbed some guy in the Henry Street Settlement on the Lower East Side who was beating a baby. We had to postpone the trial. Seems he was injured resisting arrest and spent weeks in the hospital."

I grinned. "Yeah, the baby was outmanned, so I took his side to kind of even things up. When the guy raised both hands and took a step toward me, I assumed he was attacking me. I simply defended myself."

"With a nightstick."

"Seemed like a good idea at the time."

We ordered coffee and waited. After it was served, we both sipped. Black, and very good. Sawyer leaned back and opened.

"You're working on a case that involves David Braun?"

"That's right. A missing woman. Young woman by the name of Annette Fouchet. We were hired by her mother to find her."

"And Annette's connection to Braun?"

"Boyfriend at one time ... Look, Mr. Sawyer, let me tell you about the case, what we know, and then you can ask questions, order more coffee, or leave. Fair enough?"

"Fair enough."

I gave him a pretty complete summary, including everything we knew or suspected about Braun—that he was running a brothel, probably with addicted women, and that his clientele was most likely military and longshoremen from the Brooklyn docks. I told him we suspected, but had no proof, that Annette had been addicted by Braun and might be working for him against her will, out of necessity. When I finished, he signaled the waiter for more coffee.

Sawyer sipped then cleared his throat. "I'll tell you this much: you're right about Braun running a brothel." Pause. Another sip. "I don't suppose I could convince you to back off and let this case simmer for a while, say six to eight weeks?"

Heeding Pepper's advice, I didn't say anything.

"I thought not ... And pulling your license wouldn't accomplish anything either, would it?"

I smiled.

He grunted. "Shit!" He felt in his coat pocket. Came up empty. "I don't suppose you smoke."

"Pipe."

"Figures."

"Mr. Sawyer, the FBI isn't interested in brothels so far as I know, at least not interested outside of recreational activity. And I doubt seriously if any of your guys would frequent a low-end house near the docks, anyway." He started to say something and I held up my hand. "So your interest has to be something else. What is it?"

He picked up his coffee cup, set it down, picked it up, took a sip, and set it down again. "Money and information. I'm going to level with you, Grant: we don't know his present location, where he's living or where his brothel is. We knew both, or thought we did, till a few weeks ago. He was living on Fifty-third Street and the brothel was on Sixty-first just west of Fourth Avenue. Six weeks ago, the brothel disappeared. Out of business. And he hasn't been seen at the Fifty-third Street address for a while. We have strong reasons to believe he's been supplying money and information to an organization that is, shall we say, friendly toward Hitler and the Nazis."

"When you say friendly, are you talking about the German Bund?"

"Friendlier."

"Aah, I see. As in spies."

He winced. Apparently "spies" was a no-no word, at least in public. I took out my pipe, tamped the tobacco that was in the bowl, and lit it before I said, "All right, maybe we can help each other. He had two apartments at the same time for a while. One was on Thirty-ninth Street and the other on Fifty-third, but he's moved up in the world. My information is that he's living somewhere in Bay Ridge, maybe on Sixty-eighth Street. Near the Shore Road, at any rate. I haven't located the brothel ... yet. But I will. I won't say I don't care about his other activities, but my main concern is returning Annette to her mother and aunt. How about sharing information strictly between the two of us? I can be your anonymous source. You can always call me from a pay phone."

It took him a few seconds to make up his mind. "All right. We didn't know about Thirty-ninth Street and didn't have any leads that pointed to Sixty-eighth Street. We'll check that one out, and if we confirm it, I'll call you. In the meantime, if you find the brothel, you call me. Just say you'd like to meet for coffee and I'll call back within an hour. If you specifically want to meet here, you can say Tom's. That make sense?"

"Yeah. Can the government pick up the tab here?"

Sawyer laughed. "I think we can afford it. By the way, how are you going to locate the brothel? Unlike fancy ones uptown, they don't have names, and they tend to move around."

"I have friends in low places. Beyond that, you don't want to know."

He stood up, smiling. "I guess not ... but we do have one piece of information you may not have."

"And that is?"

"The name of the madam who runs the brothel is Bertha. No last name."

I stood and thanked him. We shook hands, and he left, stopping to pay for our coffee on his way out.

Regis McCafferty

FIFTEEN

David Braun was smiling. It had been a good week. He had eight hundred to turn over to Frank in addition to two handwritten pages of information on cargo, sailings, and some of the activity going on at the army base. But that wasn't the only reason he was smiling. He was smiling at Frank's black humor in his choice of a deli to meet in. It was on Livonia just off Ninety-eighth Street on the edge of Brownsville, home to the largest concentration of Jews in the city. Given the treatment of Jews by Nazi Germany and the rumors of concentration camps, Braun doubted he'd make it back to his apartment alive if the local Jewish population knew what business he was conducting in the deli.

Frank Geiger, the man Braun met with regularly, was a native of Germany who came to the United States in 1922 and became a naturalized citizen in 1928. He was a foreman for the United States Lines in New York City, and because of his employment on the docks, he knew almost all of the other agents who were working as seamen on various ships. He received information, from Braun and others, about the sailing dates and cargoes of vessels destined for England, and then passed it on to a man Braun knew only as Paul.

Paul, sometimes known as "the cook," though Braun didn't know why, transmitted this information to Germany.

Paul was one of the prime forces in their espionage group. He arranged meetings, directed agents' activities, correlated information that had been developed, and arranged for its transmittal to Germany. Frank, who had been trained in espionage in Germany, claimed Paul was head of the German espionage system on the East Coast that tracked shipping to and from the United States.

Braun was sitting in a booth, sipping coffee, when Frank walked in, spotted him, stopped at the counter to get a coffee, and came back to the booth. As he slid in, Braun passed two envelopes across the table. Without a word, Frank picked them up, felt them, put the thicker one in his coat pocket and opened the other to take out several sheets of handwritten notes. The notes were information detailing cargoes and destinations in addition to tidbits picked up from army personnel that frequented the house. Most of the items had been collected by Bertha, but one page was Braun's. It was a fairly detailed account of some new electronic equipment that had just been received at the base. It had cost him several whiskeys with beer chasers at a bar, but the sergeant he plied with liquor seemed more than willing to brag about it.

Frank did little more than glance at the first two pages but paused at the third, the one Braun had written. He nodded his head, smiled, then went on to the last page before putting them back in the envelope and adding it to the one he'd placed in his pocket.

He took a sip of coffee then asked, "How much?"

"Eight."

"Very good, David. Paul will be pleased." He paused. "Tell me, do you have a woman who is employed in your broth—house, by the name of Annette Fouchet?"

Braun was surprised, and he showed it. "Yes, but how did you know?"

Frank ignored the question with a shrug. "Where did you meet her?"

"Saks. She was a clerk."

"But that's not where she was employed at the time you introduced her to your business, is it?"

"No, she was working at Columbia University."

"I would like to talk with her."

This was something new to Braun. Frank had never visited his brothel and had never asked to see any of the women he used. Frank was no prude, but he refrained from using common gutter terms, and rarely, if ever, swore. Thinking it might be best to have Annette looking presentable, he said, "Sure, Frank, any afternoon you like."

"No. Morning. Early morning, perhaps six thirty or so, before she gets her dose of whatever she's on. I'm tied up for the next couple days and won't be available. Let's say next Tuesday. That would be the second, I believe.

"All right. The house, or my apartment?"

"It'll have to be the house. I don't want to take a chance on her doing a runner."

"She's generally not in condition to run anywhere."
"You never know. The house. What's the address?"

Braun gave him the address and directions. Frank stood, said, "See you Tuesday about six thirty," and walked to the door.

Braun finished his coffee and lit a cigarette. After a couple minutes, he went to the counter to get a coffee to go. While waiting, he noticed an old man standing next to him. The old man stared at him for a couple seconds as if he knew him but then turned away and placed an order for coffee and two chocolate rugelach. Braun paid for his coffee and left.

SIXTEEN

It was almost two by the time I got back to the office. Pepper was on the phone and waved to me as I came in.

"Just a moment, Mr. Resnick. He just walked in." She pushed the hold button and set the phone on its cradle. "Jake Resnick, and he sounds excited."

Jake rarely called, unless it was for a bourbon and chess get-together, and that was always in the evening, so it must have been important. I walked to my desk and picked up the phone. "Yeah, Jake, you all right?"

"I'm fine, Max, but I saw your guy from the photos I developed—the one you said you slapped?"

"Where?"

"The deli I sent you to for pastries. He was sitting with another guy who left a few seconds after I came in. Your guy came up to the counter to get a coffee to go while I was standing there, so I got a good look. It was him, all right."

"I appreciate you calling, Jake. I wonder if he goes there often?"

I don't know, Max. I wouldn't have noticed him if it hadn't been for your photos. But the other guy ..."

"Yeah?"

"I swear I've seen him somewhere before, but not at the deli ... at least I don't think it was the deli. He had a look about him ..."

"What do you mean?"

"A *Mein Kampf* look. I can't explain better than that."

"You don't have to. Jake, I don't want you to go wandering the neighborhood looking for trouble, but if you see either one of them again, would you call and let us know?"

"Certainly."

"Thanks. I'll try to get around to your place one evening next week for chess and bourbon. Take care."

I took my pipe and tobacco pouch from my pocket, laid them on my desk, and hung my coat and hat on the rack. Pepper looked at me with a raised eyebrow.

I shrugged. "May or may not be something, but Jake saw Braun at a deli near his shop. He said it was undoubtedly Braun—recognized him from our photos he developed. Braun was with another guy but Jake didn't get a real good look. He thought he'd seen him before but couldn't remember where. Said he looked German, *Mein Kampf* German."

"Strange way of putting it."

"Yeah, but for Jake, I'll bet it conjures up the image of Jews being hauled off to concentration camps in Germany, and elsewhere, in just two words."

She pointed to the newspaper on her desk. "I was just reading that Britain and France have made a formal agreement that neither country will seek a separate peace with Germany. I hope we don't get involved with that mess over there."

"I hope so, too, but I don't think hoping will keep us out of it. Hitler's a crazy bastard with a huge war machine, and I doubt England and France can contain him. He has his sights set on ruling all of Europe. We pulled their chestnuts out of the fire to end the Great War in '18 and I expect we'll have to do it again."

"Not to change the subject—but to change the subject ... Murphy phoned. Wanted to know if we had any small jobs he could handle for us. He sounded bored."

"I'll call him. Today's Friday, right?"

"Yep, the twenty-ninth of March. Monday is April Fool's Day. I may fool you and not show up for work."

"You can't do that."

"Why not?"

"Partners always show up for work."

"Demote me."

"Can't do that, either."

"Why not?

"I'd have to change the sign on the door and order new business cards. Aside from that, Bo has probably made dinner plans based on your new salary, and I don't want to piss him off." I turned toward my office, grinning. "I'm going to call Murphy."

I picked up the phone, dialed, and was surprised when it rang through. Murphy had a party line, a shared line that was usually in use from one of the others on the line. He answered on the third ring.

"Hello?"

"Hello, Murph, it's Max Grant. Pepper said you called."

"Yeah, got tired of talking to my dog and Pepper has a nice voice. Actually, I was wondering if you had a bit of work for this old guy. It would keep me from waiting for my dog to talk back."

I laughed. "As it happens, Murph, I do. How about tomorrow?"

"Jeez, you working Saturdays now?"

"I am tomorrow."

"All right. What time and what will I be doing?"

"Be here by ten o'clock. Probably only four hours' work, but I'll buy lunch. We're going to be looking for a brothel in the south end of Sunset Park, not far from the Army Terminal."

"This for personal use, or business?" I couldn't see Murph's grin but could hear it in his voice.

"Do you care?"

"Nope."

"It's business. We're looking for a missing girl."

"Sounds familiar."

"I'll give you the details tomorrow, but we think she's been hooked on drugs and forced into prostitution."

"That's an old story."

"Yeah, sadly, it is. But this one may have a twist. I'll fill you in, in the morning."

"See you at ten, Max."

I looked up and Pepper was standing in the doorway. "You want me to come in tomorrow?"

"No. No need to. Murph and I are just going to wander around the Brooklyn dock area to see if we can pick up a location for Braun's brothel. With luck, we'll locate it. We can describe Annette, and one or more of the dockworkers or army guys may have used her. And that FBI agent, Sawyer, gave me the madam's name that runs the place for Braun, a woman by the name of Bertha. Don't know anything else about her."

Pepper was just about to say something when the front door of the office opened. It was Elle, with Jake from the Bowery Mission. I walked to the door between the offices, nodded at Jake with a smile, told him to grab a cup of coffee, and then turned to Elle. "Come into my office Elle, we need to talk."

She gave me an inquisitive look but walked to the side chair and sat. I went to my stash cabinet, took out a pack of Luckys and set it in front of her before I claimed my chair behind my desk. She took a cigarette from the pack, lit it with a match from the book lying on my desk, and leaned back. "So ... good news, or bad?"

"Depends. From our perspective as a detective agency, it's good. We have some leads and may be on track to find Annette. From your perspective as her mother, it's probably bad. We think—and I want to caution you that we're not certain—but we think she may have been hooked on drugs, more than likely heroin, and is being used as a prostitute in a brothel in return for a continuous supply of drugs."

She took a deep drag on the cigarette, closed her eyes, tilted her head back, and blew smoke toward the ceiling. "You know where?"

"No, not exactly, but we know the general area. I plan to go looking tomorrow with a friend of mine, a retired cop. You want to help?"

"What do you think?"

"I thought you might."

She took another drag. "When and where?"

"Here. Ten o'clock in the morning."

"Odd time to be looking for a whorehouse."

"Not really. It's somewhere near the army base and the docks. Most of those operations run twenty-four hours a day. So do the brothels."

"That makes sense." She paused. "You know who?"

"Who hooked her?"

"Yeah."

"Right now, all bets are on David Braun."

"Son of a bitch!"

I picked up my pipe. "He is that, but he may be more."

"What do you mean?"

I put a match to my pipe, and between puffs, told her what I knew about Braun's connection to a German spy ring, which, admittedly, was damned little. But I added that Braun's activities outside the brothel weren't our affair. Our interest was in getting Annette out of there and back to her mother and aunt. As I spoke, I watched her, watched her features change ever so slightly. I saw a toughness, a hardness creep into her face. Her mouth turned down slightly at the corners and her eyes narrowed. And strange as it seems, I watched her become older. Maybe I was watching her become a mother, a protective mother like a lioness with cubs, the mother she should have been. And that gave rise to another thought—regardless of the outcome with Annette, Elle might track down Braun and kill him. I wouldn't put it past her.

She stubbed out the cigarette and nodded toward Pepper's office. "Is Jake invited to the party tomorrow?"

"Of course. I'm glad he showed up with you. I'll ask him now and explain what the situation is."

"No need. I'll fill him in later at my place."

I looked up from my pipe without saying anything, but the implied question was there.

She read it. "He was at the Mission. Had thirty cents to his name. I have a warm apartment and a double bed." She paused. "I'm lonely."

"You don't have to explain to me, Elle, but I'll tell you this: he's a good man."

"I think so, too ... but thank you for saying so."

We got up and walked to the outer office where I shook hands with Jake. "Elle just volunteered your services for a job tomorrow morning. A paying job. We're going to be doing some looking around, much like we did last December when we found Sarah Bennett. She'll tell you about it later."

Elle smiled, slipped her arm inside Jake's, and turned him toward the door. "Come on, let's get some coffee and doughnuts. I'm buying."

Jake grinned. "Damn good thing. I'm busted."

As they started toward the door, Elle stopped, reached in her purse, and pulled out an envelope. She handed it to me. "It's the letter about the rubies. When I came here the other night, I told you I had a letter that would show they were mine. I'd like it back later."

"Thank you, Elle. I'll give it back to you in a day or two."

I turned to Pepper and handed her the envelope. "Read it over and then let me have it. And I'll tell ya what—it's Friday, so let's knock off for the day after you've read it. It's early enough that you can stop somewhere and pick up something good for Bo's dinner. Don't turn the phone over to the answering service; I'll do that before I leave for Ari's."

"You sure you don't need me tomorrow?"

"Yeah, I'm sure. But that reminds me, you don't have a home phone, do you?"

"No. We talked about it but haven't seen a need for one."

"Well, as a partner in this business of ours, you need one. Monday, go to the Bell Telephone office and apply for service. You'll probably have to settle for a party line at first, but while you're there, apply for a private residence line. It may take six months before you get it, but a private line is best. It's a business expense, so there's no cost to you."

"Damn good of you, boss. Oh, speaking of phones, I called Columbia to get an appointment with Professor Dunning. No dice. I talked with an assistant and was told Annette was terminated because of absenteeism and that Professor Dunning doesn't give interviews for any reason."

"Well, we may be beyond the point where anything he could tell us would help. As far as getting a phone for you is concerned, I've been thinking we should do a bit of advertising and maybe expand the business. If we do that, it's important that we stay in touch when not in the office."

I started for my desk when I heard Pepper say, "Well, that's interesting."

I turned. "What's interesting?"

She was holding the envelope in one hand and the letter in the other. "It's in French."

"Makes sense, I guess."

"I had one course in French, though years ago, but I still have the dictionary. I'll take it home with me and translate it after I tell Bo about my promotion and our new phone."

She slipped on her coat and scarf. "You're just full of surprises this week, Max. Bo will think we have something going on between us."

"God, I hope not! I have nightmares of him dangling me out the window just holding onto my ankle."

"I was just kidding. He likes you. Told me so. Besides, I'll fix him a great dinner with a good wine, and since tomorrow's Saturday, we can sleep in."

"Just out of curiosity, Pepper, how big is your bathtub?"

"Big enough, sweetie. Big enough."

She was still laughing as she went out the door. I walked into my office, stretched, sat down at my desk, picked up my pipe, and lit it. Ari wouldn't be home for several hours, probably a bit after six. That gave me time for a shower in my stand-up stall and maybe even a nap. And that's what I did.

SEVENTEEN

Bertha Much was standing near the sink, sipping coffee, when Marcia came into the kitchen, pulled out a chair, and sat at the table.

"You don't use, do you, Bertha." It was a statement, not a question.

"What do you mean?"

"I mean with all the junk that passes through this place, it's surprising you don't help yourself to a high or low."

Bertha set her coffee cup on the sink, rolled her left shirt sleeve up to show a raised scar about six inches long that started just below the bend in her arm and ran upward. It had several small raised spots about an inch apart. "Horse. I quit about four years ago."

"Damn! How'd you do that?"

"I don't know. I'm not lying; I just don't know. I'd been sick, flu or something. Fever, maybe pneumonia. Didn't see a doc. No money. Hadn't shot up for two days. Started to feel better after a couple more days and had no desire for it, none at all. Haven't had since." Bertha paused for a few seconds. "You need something now?"

Marcia shook a cigarette from her pack and lit it. "No, not just yet. I want to talk about something. More to the point, someone. My next-door neighbor, Annette."

"What about her?

"She doesn't belong here."

Bertha let out a laugh that sounded more like a bark. "She didn't walk in the front door and ask for a job. She rode the horse—same way you did. Or maybe it was coke, or maybe both. Don't make no difference."

"Maybe from your point of view it doesn't make any difference, but from mine it does. You and I have been around, know the score, just like most or maybe all the girls here, except Annette. I was using before I met Braun, though it was hit and miss, and I suspect that's true of most of the others. Hell, Braun was a godsend. He provided a regular supply till he cut us off. Then he made the offer: work for him in exchange for an unlimited supply, as long as what we used didn't interfere with screwing, or whatever the customer wanted.

"But Annette was different. She never used before she met him. I'm not even sure she'd ever been to bed with a man before Braun. He turned her, turned her inside out. He's one corrupt son of a bitch and he corrupted her. You know that, Bertha, and so do I. And that's what makes the difference."

Bertha added some coffee to her cup, shuffled to the table in her slippers, and sat down. Her voice was soft, low. "If I were you, Marcia, I wouldn't be saying things like that to anyone else. I'm surprised you said it to me."

A hint of a smile played on Marcia's face. "You don't like Braun any more than I do. But I understand why you're here. You have a decent place to stay, food on the table, and what I assume is a pretty good salary. That's hard to walk away from. You're hooked as much as I am."

"Not quite. I *can* walk away. You can't." Bertha set her cup on the table. "You can't unless you want to suffer the runny nose and eyes, diarrhea, nausea, pain in every part of your body, the bottomless despair ... I've been there—you've been there. How many times have you thought of just ending it all?"

Marcia took a deep drag on her cigarette and blew the smoke toward the ceiling. "Let me tell you, Bertha: you'd better believe I could cut out of here whenever I want to, and I'd dare you to try to stop me. But I also know the consequences, and the question is whether it's a fair trade. I don't know that yet."

Bertha lifted her cup then set it down without drinking. "Even if you did decide to try to leave here, dry out, David wouldn't like it. He'd stop you."

"And I'd disappear like some of the other women who have vanished from here, huh?"

Bertha's head snapped up. "What have you heard? Who told you about any of the girls disappearing?"

"Bullshit, Bertha! You know all about it. You'd have to. The girls notice. They talk. Three disappeared a couple weeks ago, not at the same time, but over two days. Two were pretty well used up from what I heard. I don't know about the other one. Maybe she was a troublemaker. And it was Braun who made sure they disappeared, didn't he?"

"I don't know what happened to them."

"Yeah, but you can guess, can't you? I can guess, too. I think Braun offed them and got rid of the bodies somehow. If he ever gets nailed for that, you'll be implicated as an accomplice. If you're lucky, you'll only get twenty years, maybe at Elmira, maybe Westfield State Farm if the court is lenient. I figure you're near fifty now. You'd be about seventy when you got out, even if you lived through it, and that's a rough age to start over."

"Gimme one of your cigarettes."

Marcia said nothing, but slid the pack over with a box of matches.

Bertha took one, lit it, and coughed. "What do you want?"

"I want your help getting Annette out of here and into a hospital."

"Can't—he'd kill me!"

"Not if I kill the bastard first." Marcia smirked. "Just kidding." She wasn't kidding but doubted she'd ever have the opportunity.

"How would you get her out? What would I have to do?"

"I haven't figured it all out yet, but you could start by tapering off her heroin. Not cut off completely, just smaller doses. Same with the coke if she asks for it. You gave her three days off to recover from some rough treatment. She has two to go. That will take her through Sunday night. Go light on her Monday. Use her only if you have to. Maybe I can get her out of here on Tuesday. I'll talk with her later and let you know."

"What else?"

"She'll have to get out and can't use the front door because of the alarm you set when we close business about two in the morning. And you have to set it. If you don't and Braun finds out, you're done here, or done for good. You and Braun are the only ones with a key, and you don't key it to the off position till nine o'clock or so. That's too late. I want her out of here by seven. You're going to have to give me a crowbar or jemmy so I can break the lock on the metal bar at the back door. That will cover your ass with Braun. If you just opened the door for us, he would know you had something to do with it. Whatever you give me, I'll take with me and hide it somewhere so he won't tie it to you."

"Anything else?"

"Yeah, one more thing. If you go to Braun with this, I'll hammer you. I'll lie, I'll screw him, I'll do whatever it takes, but I'll live to get you. You may run this place, but I'm a valuable commodity of his. He may beat me around, but he isn't going to kill me off. Not just yet, anyway. Do you understand?

Bertha smashed her cigarette out in the ashtray. "Yeah, I understand."

"Good. Now get your kit. You can fix me up."

EIGHTEEN

Sometimes an hour's nap leaves me foggy, sometimes bright-eyed and bushy tailed. This evening was foggy. And a glance out the window while getting dressed told me it was as foggy outside as inside. But that made the transportation decision an easy one. Ari lived on Hinsdale and that meant a bus ride to Ninety-eighth and Dumont, and then a trolley to Hinsdale. I enjoyed the bus and trolley, enjoyed watching the hustle-bustle of people rushing to and fro on the sidewalks or going in and out of stores. Down-and-outs would gather at the bus or trolley stops and panhandle for what they could get. They figured if a person had enough to ride, they might spare a dime. In some areas, a dime would get you a cup of coffee and a doughnut. Or five dimes would buy a pint of cheap wine. But this evening, I'd take a taxi.

I like taxis almost as much as I like public transportation, but taxi drivers are hit and miss. There are silent ones, talkative ones, some who play the radio, and others who won't unless you ask them. Occasionally, I've run into an intellectual type. A couple months ago, I had a driver who wanted to talk about Einstein's theory of relativity. The astonishing thing was that he really sounded like he knew what he was talking about. I didn't.

I dressed then went into my office to phone Ari. She picked up on the third ring.

"Hello?"

"Hi there, gorgeous. It's your favorite detective. What's for dinner?"

"What are you hungry for?"

"You."

"I'm blushing."

"I doubt it."

She laughed. "Just something quick."

"That's for later."

"I hope not."

"Hope not what?"

"Quick."

"Ye gads, woman! I'm hungry!"

"Fresh coffee, scrambled eggs, home fries, and ham."

"I'm on my way. Love you."

"Love you, too."

I considered whether to take my .38 with me. Decided against it. Changed my mind two minutes later, put my belt holster on and slipped my snubby into it. I didn't expect trouble of any kind, but it seems every time I don't expect any difficulty, it arrives like the plague. I stopped at my stash cabinet, took out a fresh pipe and a pouch of Edgeworth tobacco. My old Irish walking hat, brim down all the way round, and my scarf went on before my raincoat. Then I paused to look around the office to see if I was forgetting anything. I was. I went to my desk, took Elle's postcard photo out, along with one of the photo copies of Annette, put them in my inside coat pocket and headed out the door.

There was a light but very cold rain coming down in the fog, so I stood in the building alcove watching for a taxi coming south on Flatbush. Didn't have long to wait. I spotted an empty, walked to the curb, and flagged. When it stopped, I hopped in the back and at the "Where to" gave her Ari's address. Yeah—her. We don't have many women cab drivers in the city, but do have some. I looked at her ID pinned to the passenger side sun visor. Milly Kovacs.

"Radio?" She had a gravelly voice.

"Nah, just the ride."

"Suits me." She cracked her window an inch and lit a cigarette.

Tit for tat. I filled and lit my pipe. The smoke drifted forward and out her window. I watched the world go by, what I could see of it. Vague shapes moved along the sidewalk in the fog and it was hard to tell man from woman. The fog was getting thicker as we moved north. I thought that strange because we were moving away from the upper bay and Hudson River, but it happens.

We made a hard stop as a traffic light turned red just in front of us. My cabbie rolled down the window a bit more and pitched her cigarette. "What kind of tobacco you smoking in that pipe?"

"Edgeworth."

"Smells good. Better than my—"

A body slammed against the cab at the driver's side back door, the opposite side from where I was sitting. I thought at first it was someone who had misjudged their distance because of the fog, but they slammed again. It was a woman, and some guy was doing a number on her by banging her against the cab.

As I got out of the taxi, I said to the cabbie, "Don't move!"

I moved around to the back of the cab, slipped my hand inside my jacket and rested it on my .38. "Hey, Bud, knock it off!"

He actually stopped mid-push and looked at me. "Piss off, Jock, before you take her place."

"Try me."

He let go of her and she slowly slid down the side of the cab to the pavement. He was a big brute, bigger than me, and fists raised, he took three steps toward me. I let him get just shy of arm's length before I cleared leather, arm forward, and his forehead smacked up against my snubnose.

I'm good at growling, so I growled. "Keep pushing, Bud, and I'll turn your head into a drainage ditch." He froze and I swear his eyes crossed as he looked at my gun. Then he backed off a foot.

I kept the gun on him and growled some more. "Now be a good little boy and go to the sidewalk."

He stood there for a few seconds, debating God knows what, looked at the gun again, shrugged, and disappeared into the fog toward the curb. Still looking in the direction he'd gone, I went to the woman on the ground, took hold of her arm, and helped her to her feet. I opened the door of the taxi and simply said, "Get in."

She did, and slumped at an angle across the back seat. I went back around the cab, still keeping my eyes peeled in the general direction her attacker went, got in, holstered my .38, slammed the door, and told Milly to take off. And we did, but at no more than twenty miles per hour.

I leaned to my left, took hold of the woman by the shoulders, and straightened her up. She moaned. Her eyes were closed, but in the dim light, I could see her face. Her left cheek and forehead were red, scraped, and her bottom lip was split in the middle. Bozo had worked her over before deciding to try to break bones by slamming her into my cab.

She moaned again, but opened her eyes. Her voice was soft, ragged, not much more than a croak. "Thanks, mister."

I nodded. "You want to go to a hospital?"

"No ... No. Where are we?"

"In this pea soup, I'm not sure." I leaned forward. "Milly?"

"Coming up on Ninety-eighth Street."

The woman looked at me for a couple seconds. Then she asked, "Brownsville?"

"Yeah, Brownsville, or close."

"You can let me out at Ninety-eighth. I appreciate what you done, mister. I thought that goddam asshole was going to kill me."

"So did I. You know him?"

"Sorta." She didn't elaborate.

I didn't pursue it. "What's your name?"

She hesitated, but finally said, "Vivian ... Vivian Spaulding. Really. That's my real name. What's yours?"

"Max Grant." I took one of my cards from my shirt pocket and gave it to her. She glanced at it then put it in her coat pocket.

I'm pretty good at hunches, and I had one. "Vivian?"

"Yeah?"

"Do you ever get over to the Brooklyn docks or around the army base?"

She turned her head sharply toward me and winced with the effort. "Why?"

"I'm working on a case and looking for a woman named Bertha who runs a brothel in that area."

She started to say something, hesitated. For a fraction of a second, I thought I saw fear flash in her eyes. Then she turned her head forward. "No I don't know any Bertha."

Milly pulled to the curb. "Ninety-eighth Street."

I opened the door and got out, and Vivian followed but leaned against the cab as she did.

I reached out my hand to steady her. "You sure you're all right?"

She took a couple steps. "Yeah, I'm sure. Thanks again, Mr. Grant."

"You're welcome, Vivian. You take care."

I got back in the taxi and we drove off. Milly turned her head slightly. "Hooker?"

"Probably." I took my pipe from my pocket and lit it again. "Doesn't make any difference. I don't like to see some guy beating a woman."

"I didn't know you were packin' a gun."

"Neither did Vivian's goddamn asshole."

We both laughed.

When we pulled over in front of Ari's apartment building, I paid the fare with a bit extra in the tip for Milly. She reached for her clipboard, wrote something on a slip of paper and handed it to me. "That's the taxi office supervisor's number. If you want me for something special, just ask for Milly. He'll get hold of me." She smiled. "Hauling you around is an adventure."

I smiled back and started to get out, but stopped with one foot on the sidewalk. I'd had another one of those "out of the blue" thoughts. "You get many fares in or around the army depot, the Sunset Park area?"

"Some ... more often evening than daytime and more often after payday at the army base. Any place specific?"

In for a penny, in for a pound, as they say. "Yeah, you might have overheard me say something to Vivian ... I'm looking for a brothel, a particular brothel. And before you ask, its business."

"I don't cruise that area, and in any case, the brothels don't have names, just reputations. I maybe know of three or four, but they occasionally move from location to location. You have any sort of description?"

"No. All I have is the name of the woman who runs the place. Bertha."

"Doesn't ring a bell. Let me have your phone number and I'll ask around. I'll call if I pick up something from another driver."

I gave her one of my cards, thanked her, and exited the cab. The fog was beginning to lift a bit, or at least I thought so. I could see the steps leading up to the alcove of Ari's apartment building and could make out the outline of the doorway. I stepped into the alcove and rang the buzzer for 2B. After a few seconds, her voice came over the intercom.

"Yes?"

"It's just a poor homeless, starving detective in need of coffee, scrambled eggs, home fries, and ham."

"Did you say homeless or helpless?"

"Take your pick."

"Helpless."

"That'll do."

"That's good. I feel domineering."

"Does that mean I can take a nap while you're on top?"

"Shit!"

"I guess that means no, huh?"

No reply. The door clicked open and I went up the stairs.

She was standing at her front door wearing the pale yellow knee-length dress with blue piping around the low-cut neck that I hadn't seen since the first day we met. Back then, I wanted to say, "Hello, delicious," but didn't. This time I did, then followed it up with an embrace and a kiss. And she was delicious. I marveled at every time I saw or held her.

As she closed the door behind us she pointed to the closet. "Coat and hat, and then come into the kitchen. Dinner in about three minutes."

I obeyed. What guy wouldn't? Besides, dirty old man that I am, I was thinking of after dinner. The kitchen was small, but big enough for a table with two chairs. Ari poured me a cup of coffee as I sat down.

She turned back to the eggs, smiling. "So, Mr. Grant, what's new in the detecting world? More to the point, is David Braun involved in the disappearance of Annette Fouchet?"

"I think so. Let's put it this way: I'm ninety-nine percent sure he is, but he's involved in a lot more than that, and all of it about as nasty as it gets."

"Like what?"

"Drugs, prostitution, running a brothel, connections with German spies, and for all I know, murder."

She turned from the stove toward me with her mouth open. "Really? Are you serious?"

"Boy Scout's honor."

She fixed two plates, set one in front of me, and then sat down herself. "David Braun? The David Braun that worked for us? Tell me about it."

So I told her ... between bites. I told her we believed Braun hooked women on drugs, and in order to support their habit, forced them into prostitution at a brothel he ran. Some of those women had worked at Saks, but that was probably just one of several sources for Braun. Without mentioning my FBI connection, I told her that some of Braun's income from the brothel, along with information the women gathered from dockworkers and servicemen, probably supported one or more German spy networks operating in the city. And finally, I told her that since Braun was dating Annette before she disappeared, we were assuming she was now one of his prostitutes. We had no proof as yet, but my gut told me it was as close to a sure bet as I could get.

She had stopped eating. "Annette is such a sweet young thing ..."

Regis McCafferty

"And that's why he went after her. Young, naïve, inexperienced girls have to be a draw at a brothel, particularly in an area where a substantial number of your customers are servicemen. We're convinced, or at least I'm convinced, that Braun's running his operation near the Brooklyn docks not far from the military installation, but hopefully, we'll know more after tomorrow."

"What's going on tomorrow?"

"Me, Murphy, Elle, and Jake are going to wander the area tomorrow morning. Try to pick up information and locate the brothel."

"Jake?"

"Jake from the Bowery Mission. Remember? He helped us find Sarah Bennett back in December. He knows Elle, so there's a connection. Aside from that, he's a good fellow to have around." I smiled. "He has a knack for picking locks."

After dinner, we went to the living room with our coffee, and I retrieved my pipe from my coat pocket before we sat side by side on the couch. I had also taken Elle's postcard from my pocket and handed it to Ali before lighting my pipe.

She looked at it for a full thirty seconds before saying anything. "I wonder when Annette had this photo taken. The setting looks quite old, so it must have been in a studio."

"The resemblance is remarkable, isn't it? That's Annette's mother, Elle. But you're right about the studio. It was taken twenty-five years ago in Paris, France."

"My God! They could be twin sisters! What's Elle look like now?"

"About the same, but older. A good-looking woman for her middle forties when you consider the life she's led. She returned to the States from France several months ago. Probably a good thing, because all indications are that Germany may invade France in the not-too-distant future. She'd be trapped there if she stayed."

"Hitler *ist Scheisse!*"

I laughed. "Yeah, Hitler is shit. I got that. But it isn't going to change anything. What little I read in the newspapers tells me he's on the move in Europe and there's no one to stop him. But my primary concern is getting Annette back to her mother. If it turns out I take Braun out of the picture and put a crimp in some Nazi spy plans, all well and good, but that's not what Elle hired me for."

"If I remember correctly, you managed to mess up some Nazi plans when you rescued Sarah Bennett."

"Yeah, but they were the ones holding her. Besides, it was personal. I owed them a hard time."

Smiling, she put her hand on my thigh. "Speaking of hard time ... I'll stack the dishes while you finish your pipe and coffee. I'll meet you in the bedroom."

What could I say to that? Nothing. I just smiled, took a sip of coffee, and relit my pipe. She got up and headed to the kitchen. I sat for a few minutes, sipping coffee and slowly smoking my pipe, savoring the aroma of a nutty-tasting semi-sweet tobacco, before going to the kitchen to add my cup to the stack.

She was just slipping into bed when I entered the bedroom. I got in bed behind her and moved my right hand down between her legs. Without saying a word, I nuzzled and kissed her neck. She turned, placed her hand between my legs and gently massaged, which got an immediate reaction. She put her lips close to my ear and whispered, "Mr. Grant, I think you're going to give me a hard time."

"You betcha, lady."

She pushed me back, rolled on top straddling me, raised a little, and put her hand between my legs. We moved together, slowly, savoring the lovemaking till we reached an intense orgasm together. She trembled, then nestled her head against my neck.

"So, mister hard guy," I could hear the smile in her voice, "what time do you have to be up in the morning?"

"Which *up* are we talking about?"

"The second one."

"In time for a bath. I have to meet the folks at ten."

"Hmm ... I'll set the alarm for six thirty."

"That'll work."

As I drifted off, I knew, as certain as if it were carved in stone, that this, this feeling of completeness and belonging, is what was meant by being in love.

NINETEEN

I took a taxi back to my office. I was running a bit slow after my second "up" of the morning but managed to make it by nine o'clock. As I walked to my office past Pepper's desk, I noticed a copy of the *Philadelphia Enquirer*. It was several days old, March 24th to be exact, and I would have expected headlines dealing with the war in Europe. Instead, in large bold letters, was the headline.

REBELLIOUS I.R.A. CONVICTS PUT TORCH TO DARTMOOR; TWO WARDENS HELD CAPTIVE.

Since it generally takes some doing to knock Hitler off the front page, and one would hardly think it would be the Irish Republican Army to do it, I decided to take a look, so I picked it up.

PRINCETON, England, March 23 (U.P.)—Smoke and flames poured from Dartmoor Prison for two hours today after Irish Republican Army prisoners set their cell block afire, bound and gagged their wardens and ran riot through parts of the penitentiary.

The I.R.A. convicts, celebrating the anniversary of the famous Dublin Easter Rebellion, were subdued only after Devonshire county police had been rushed to the prison.

The outbreak was reported to have been started by 19 I.R.A. convicts who gave the signal for rioting during a teatime by singing and jeering.

The prison chaplain, it was understood, intervened and influenced the rioters to abandon the disturbance, making it possible for guards to restore order.

And further down the column, Sherlock Holmes makes an entrance, though not by name:

Dartmoor—near the scenes in The Hound of the Baskervilles—*is in Devonshire, and the country's toughest prisoners are sent there ...*

So there you have it, I thought. Tea works as well to incite the Irish as their whiskey. The European conflict did make a few column headers further down the page with Mussolini celebrating the twenty-first anniversary of Fascism in Italy, Hitler meeting with Molotoff, and the Vatican voicing pessimism on the outlook for early peace. There was a single, short column that stated *TOKIO NAVY CALLED READY FOR U.S. RISE.* Some admiral named Mitsumasa Yonai said the Japanese Navy is ready to meet any situation resulting from the current expansion of the United States Navy. News to me. I didn't know we were expanding our Navy, and what the hell that had to do with the Japanese was beyond me. I joke with Pepper that my knowledge of the Far East is confined to what I learn from the *Terry and the Pirates* comic strip in the Sunday paper, but given their rabid aggression in China, the Japanese bear watching. And I remembered reading that the United States terminated their trade agreement with Japan in January of this year, cutting off cotton, oil, and steel. That probably pissed them off.

I shrugged, set the paper back on Pepper's desk, and busied myself fixing a pot of coffee. There was a chill in the air this morning, and I figured my gang of three could use a cup when they showed up. Before going to my desk, I went to the floor safe and took out forty bucks in ones and fives to cover today's expenses.

Murphy was the first one in. I was sitting at my desk, looking at a map of Brooklyn while enjoying a cup of coffee and my second pipe of the day, when he came through the door.

"Fresh coffee in the pot, Murph."

"Thank you, lad. It's a bit brisk this morning." He poured a cup then came into the office and stood to one side of the desk looking at the map. "Looks familiar."

"Yeah, but we'll be looking at an area a bit farther south than last December. Primarily Sunset Park near the docks, though I may stray into Bay Ridge."

I heard the main office door open. "That's probably the rest of our crew."

It was. Elle and Jake came into my office and I made introductions, though Jake and Murph knew each other from the Sarah Bennett case.

I gave a brief but comprehensive sketch of the case, more for Murph's benefit, but also for Jake because I didn't know what Elle had told him. As I handed Jake and Elle a copy of Annette's photo, I added, "I don't expect to find Annette today but what I'm hoping is we can find the brothel I think she's being held in." Elle winced, but didn't say anything. "Chances are the prostitutes don't get out much, if at all, but the name of the woman who runs the place is Bertha. If we can get a line on her, and identify the house, that's as much as we can expect today. Then we can—"

Elle interrupted, anger in her voice. "If we find the goddamn house, why can't we just go in and get my daughter?"

"Because we have to somehow confirm she's there. We only suspect it now. If we force our way in, it could mean trouble. Believe it or not, they could call the cops. Most of the brothels in the area exist because the police, or at least some of them, turn a blind eye to the business. Maybe they do it because they have more important things on their menu, or maybe some are being paid off. It doesn't make any difference. We don't need the hassle or interference. So, here's the plan: Identify the house. Confirm Annette is there. Get her out. Sounds simple. It isn't. Just locating the brothel is going to take legwork and luck. Once we do, we'll lay out a plan for the rest, and I have some ideas how that can be done.

"So here's how we're going to play this today: We're going to have to hit the local bars because it's more likely that's where we'll find dockworkers and army guys who patronize brothels. Jake, you and Elle will be husband and wife looking for Elle's younger sister who came to the big city from somewhere else. Make something up. That'll work better than searching for a daughter. Why? Because searching for a daughter is too emotional, not only for the guy you may be talking with but also for you, Elle. You can show the photo of Annette if you need to. It would be logical for you to have one. Murph, you and I will separate and check out different bars. We won't show a photo or ask about Annette, but simply ask questions about a brothel that moved from farther north in Sunset Park. We can say it had some fine girls but all we remember is that Bertha was the name of the woman who ran the place."

Elle reached in her bag, pulled out a loose cigarette, and lit it. "All right, where do we start?"

"We'll take a taxi from here to Sunset Park at Forty-fourth and Seventh Avenue. You and Jake will work the bars from there to the dock and keep moving south a block at a time. Murph, I'll drop you on Fifty-eighth Street, and you can work the same way north. I'm going to go farther south to Bay Ridge and wander around a bit. I have a tip that Braun is living in that area. Chances of spotting him are slim, but I might get lucky. If I don't, I'll start working north from Sixty-sixth Street. Jake, here's twenty bucks, and the same for you, Murph. That should cover drinks and a bite to eat if you get hungry. It should also cover buying a beer for some guy if you think you're onto something. Go light on your own drinking. Sip. You won't come off as serious if you're zonked. There are probably two to three dozen bars in that whole area and I doubt we can get to them all, so we may be doing the same thing on Monday. Take a taxi back here. I should be here before five o'clock."

I paused for a few seconds. "Look, I think chances are slim that we find the brothel, but there's still that chance. I don't know of any other way but legwork, so let's get going." I took my peacoat and watch cap from the rack and herded everyone toward the front door. My .38 was on my belt. Prudent.

I was lying when I said I didn't know of another way to locate the brothel. I did, but it was a last resort, something to be kept in reserve. I could ask Elle to walk the streets and talk with the freelance prostitutes. From what I knew or suspected, it was unlikely any had worked for Braun or Bertha, but word gets around and they may have heard of the place. But I preferred not to suggest it ... for the moment.

TWENTY

I dropped Jake and Elle off at Forty-fourth and Seventh Avenue then Murph at Fifty-eighth Street and had the cabbie head south to the corner of Bay Ridge Avenue and Fourth Avenue. I headed west on Bay Ridge, walking at a normal pace, and simply looking over the neighborhood. The weather was cool, overcast, but decent. At least no rain.

At one time, Bay Ridge was the home of elegant mansions and the wealthy, with Shore Road, overlooking the bay, being the most exclusive property. That gradually changed with the arrival of the Fourth Avenue subway. The population increased dramatically, primarily with Scandinavians and Italians, and the mansions were replaced by a mix of row houses and apartments with the occasional single home, usually at the corner of an intersecting street.

A little more than halfway between Third Avenue and Colonial Road, there were two small girls playing hopscotch. I stopped for a moment to watch and then noticed something odd. Most hopscotch patterns, that I remembered, were chalked out with eight or ten squares. This one had nine. Curious, I asked one of the girls why they didn't have ten squares. Her reply?

"Simple, mister. We ran out of chalk." I smiled, nodded my head, and then walked on, feeling like a dummy.

Unlike the other folks, I wasn't looking for a bar. Hell, I wasn't sure what I was looking for. I didn't expect Braun to pop out of the woodwork. In fact, the last thing I wanted was to be seen by him. He'd remember the slapping incident for sure, and what might happen then would be unpredictable. Worse—it could screw up getting Annette out of his brothel, if that's where she was, and I wasn't too damned sure of that.

At Shore Road, I turned right and walked to Sixty-eighth Street where I turned right again and headed back toward Fourth Avenue. About halfway into the second block was a small deli, and I thought about stopping for a cup of coffee, but decided against it. With my luck, Braun would wander in and I'd be trapped. I decided to put off coffee till I'd worked my way farther north. If that manager I'd talked with a couple days before was right—and for the ten bucks I'd paid him, I was hoping he was—Braun had moved to Sixty-eighth Street. I was plodding along, telling myself that at least I was getting some exercise, when halfway between Colonial Road and Ridge Boulevard I spotted it. Well ... maybe. In front of a very nice and well-kept apartment building was a '39 Ford Coupe, medium gray. It was on the opposite side of the street, facing me. I kept walking but noted the address of the apartment. It could be coincidence, but odds were, it wasn't.

I'd walked to the end of the block when, on impulse, I turned to look back. A man and woman had come out of the apartment building and were walking toward the gray coupe. He was less than medium height and slightly built. She was wearing a small round hat but I could see she had long blonde hair. As much as I wanted it to be Braun, I couldn't tell for sure at this distance. I put the odds of it being Braun at about five-to-one in favor, but I wouldn't bet my life on it. Still, it felt right. I'd seen enough to satisfy me. I cut across the street and started walking north to Sixty-fifth street and local bars.

I stopped in four bars, staying for little more than a half hour in each, before calling it quits for the day. They were a bust, but I stayed long enough in the second one to have a sandwich with my beer. The name of the place was Feathers. Of course, I walked in looking for feathers hanging from the ceiling or mounted on the wall. None to be seen. I took a seat at the bar and ordered a Stroh's. Working man's beer. Fire brewed, or so their advertising said. The bar had a one-page menu in a plastic slip cover. I glanced at it, picked out a sandwich, then noticed a line at the bottom: "Joseph Feathers, Proprietor." Solved that problem.

I only wished the problem of Annette could be solved as easily. I must have talked with a dozen guys and none of them knew of a whorehouse madam named Bertha. I looked the part of a merchant seaman with my beat-up peacoat and ratty watch cap, and my storyline was fair, or at least believable. I was in between ships, laying off onshore for a couple months, and was looking for a house and a whore I'd visited several months ago, but it had moved. Some of the guys I talked with could easily name a whorehouse and give directions, but not Bertha's place.

I got back to my office a bit after four o'clock, hung up my hat and coat, and debated fixing another pot of coffee. Figured I'd better. I pitched the old stuff, rinsed the pot, loaded it up, turned the burner on, and went to my desk to light the pipe that was still sitting in the ashtray. I sat as well. It was more afterthought than anything, but I decided to call our answering service for any messages.

"City Message Service, could I have your phone number, please?"

I gave it.

"One message. You'd better write it down because it doesn't make much sense. No callback number given, either."

"Just a sec." I picked up a pencil and moved a pad in front of me. "Go ahead."

"Fifty-first Street between Ninth and Tenth. Unattached brownstone. Green door. Bertha. Thanks again, Vivian."

I stared at what I'd written. "I'll be a son of a bitch!"

"What was that, sir?"

"I'm sorry. Nothing, nothing at all. Thank you. I understand it."

I hung up. Aloud, I said, "Vivian Spaulding, I could kiss you. And if you were here, I would. Wait till I tell—" I stopped. Better think this through. Vivian had given me the location of Braun's brothel. If I told the crew that I expected any minute, they'd want to go now, particularly Elle. Not a good idea, at least not without a bit of planning. It's one thing to visit a whorehouse for the intended purpose. It's quite another to hit one with the purpose of busting someone out, and a drug addict, to boot. No telling what kind of shape Annette would be in or what sort of opposition we'd run into. Hell, for all I knew, Bertha could be packing a pistol, Braun could be there, probably armed, or they may have bouncers on the premises. No, I need to know more. Best keep my mouth shut about Vivian's message.

The coffee had been perking for a couple minutes. Long enough. I got up, walked to the pot and turned off the burner just as the office door opened. It was Murphy—alone. He looked at me and shrugged.

"No luck, Max, not even a hint. How 'bout you?"

"Nothing solid. I did spot a '39 Ford coupe on Sixty-eighth that could be Braun's, and saw a man and woman get into it, but I was too far away to be sure it was him. In any case, it was an upscale apartment block and not a place we'd likely find a brothel. Did you see Jake and Elle?"

"Nope. I quit after four streets and seven bars. Stopped for a sandwich and coffee at a drug store lunch counter on Fifty-fifth and then hit the last two bars just shy of the docks. Hell, I had to walk back to Seventh Avenue to get a taxi."

A plan had started to form in my mind as Murph was talking. Vague, but maybe an approach to confirm if Annette was in the brothel. I picked up a cup, poured, and handed it to him. "You going to be free Monday and Tuesday?"

"Yep. Whatcha have in mind?"

"Not sure yet, but don't mention anything to Jake and Elle."

"Whatever you say, boss. You onto something?"

"Just a hunch for now. Can you be here at three in the afternoon, Monday?"

"I'll be here."

Just then the office door opened and in walked Jake and Elle, both looking tired and dejected. I pointed to the coffee pot. "It's fresh. Looks like you could use some."

Elle picked up a cup. "Got something to go in it?"

I went to my office, to my stash cabinet, took out a bottle of bourbon, returned to the outer office and handed it to Elle. She poured more than a dollop in two cups, filled them with coffee, and handed one to Jake before taking a seat in Pepper's chair. She took a sip, grimaced, took another sip—no grimace—then looked up at me. "You know how many bars there are in that area?"

"Nope."

"Neither do I, but there are too goddamn many. I lost track after six."

Jake sipped and smiled. "We managed to get to ten. We quit on Fifty-second Street about a block short of the docks. I'm not sure there were any bars left on Fifty-second, but at the time, I didn't care. You have any luck? Either of you?"

Murph shook his head no, but I answered for both of us. "Murph got as far north as Fifty-fifth Street and I got to Sixty-fourth, but the only thing of interest I saw was what might be Braun's Ford Coupe. I saw a man and woman get into it but was too far away to tell if it was Braun. Could have been anyone."

Elle set the cup down. "So what now, Mr. Detective?"

I sensed a bit of snide in the question, but ignored it. "Tomorrow is Sunday and it would be a waste to spend our time in the area. Bars are closed, and for all I know, so are the brothels. Once upon a time, I was a member of New York's finest. Murphy knows that, but I don't think you two do." I nodded to Elle and Jake. "Monday, I may contact a cop I know to see if he can provide some information. Remember, we're working on an assumption that Annette's been forced into working in a brothel. That assumption is mine, based on what I know, past experience, and gut feeling. And it could be wrong. I don't think it is but the possibility exists. For now, let's plan on meeting here Tuesday afternoon, say three o'clock. If I get some solid information Monday from the sergeant I know, I'll call you."

Elle listened, nodded her head yes, but I could tell she didn't like it. Poor mother she had been, she was still a mother on a mission. She took Jake's cup and set them both on Pepper's desk. "All right, we'll wait to hear from you. Would you do me one favor? No matter what you hear from your cop friend, or if you hear nothing on Monday, would you call me?"

"Yes, I promise. Do you have money left over from the twenty I gave you?"

Jake checked his pocket. "Yeah, eleven bucks and some change."

"Keep it and treat yourself to a meal this evening."

Jake smiled, nodded thanks, and ushered Elle out the door. After waiting a few seconds, I walked to the door, opened it a crack and could hear Jake and Elle going down the stairs. I closed the door and turned to Murph. "You're right. I may have a lead and maybe a good one. We'll know Monday. I hate to cut Elle out of this—hell, it's her daughter—but I'm afraid she'd blow it. And I have to think it through ... come up with some plan I think will work. At any rate, show up Monday afternoon, and bring your revolver."

"Will do, Max. Want me to wash up the cups?"

"Nah, I'll do it before I leave. Anything left of the twenty I gave you?" "Most of it. Hell, at a dime for a short beer, twenty goes a long way."

"All right, keep it. And Murph, thanks for being here. I appreciate it."

I finished my coffee, washed the pot and cups, then went to my desk, lit my pipe, and sat. I was mulling over an idea I had that might just confirm Annette was in the brothel. I've never been a client of a whorehouse, but there's a first for everything, or so they say. But for what I had in mind, I'd need Murphy and Pepper. Well, I'd work out the details by Monday afternoon.

I picked up the phone and dialed Ari's number.

"Hello?"

"You hungry?"

"I will be by the time you get here."

"How about dinner and a movie? My treat. You pick 'em. I'm too tired to make major decisions."

"How soon will you be here?"

The Nude on the Postcard

"An hour, maybe a bit more."

"I'll be ready. Love you.

"Love you too, Ari."

I showered, changed clothes, caught a taxi to Ari's, and was there in little over an hour. She was waiting for me just outside the apartment building door, so I asked the driver to wait. As she came down the steps, she said, "Tell him he can go, Max. We'll walk."

I paid the diver and took Ari by the arm. "Where to, lady?"

"Just a couple blocks to a small Italian restaurant named Tony's. Family place. Good table wine, salads, and rigatoni to die for. I think it has pepperoni in it."

"Sounds great. I'm starved. And the movie?"

"Well ... I thought about *Wuthering Heights* with Laurence Olivier and Merle Oberon, but it might be too heavy, so I opted for *Mr. Smith goes to Washington* with Jimmy Stewart and Jean Arthur. It's being shown at the Lowes on Pitkin Avenue here in Brownsville. It's kind of a serious comedy about political corruption."

"That's what it is, all right."

"What?"

"Political corruption. A serious comedy played by serious crooked politicians."

As Ari said, the rigatoni was excellent, and we were served by the owner, who had a pronounced Italian accent. When he brought the spumoni for dessert, I thanked him.

"Excellent dinner, Tony. Best rigatoni I've ever had."

"Ima glad you lika, sir. My wifa da cook."

As he moved away from our table, Ari leaned toward me and whispered. "His name isn't Tony, It's Myron— Myron Stein. Jewish, of course. Oh, he was born in Italy, Milan I think, but came to America about ten years ago. He just thought 'Tony's' would sound better for an Italian restaurant than 'Myron's.'"

I chuckled. "I agree. What time does the movie start?"

"8:30. We have time to walk. it's not far."

It wasn't, and the movie was one of the best I've seen in a long time. It was just the right mix of comedy and drama. Jimmy Stewart played the lead with an excellent cast of Jean Arthur, Edward Arnold, and Claude Rains. Rains is one of my favorite actors but in this film played a corrupt politician.

Afterward, we walked back to Ari's apartment, and over hot cocoa and apple pie, we laughed when recalling some of the movie. We moved to the living room after refilling our cups. As Ari sat down next to me she said, "There was comedy, but even the comedy was serious at times."

I took a sip of cocoa and smiled. "Remember that part toward the end where Jimmy Stewart is defending himself against false charges and has taken to the floor of the Senate to speak? He was asked to yield and refused." Then, in my best Jimmy Stewart imitation, which was lousy, I said, "No, sir, I'm afraid not, no sir. I yielded the floor once before, if you can remember, and I was practically never heard of again."

We both laughed again as we had in the theater. I reached over to the end table, picked up my pipe, lit it, took a couple puffs and then set it in the ashtray. "I love being with you, Ari, particularly after a day like today. It was frustrating but maybe we got a break. Not sure yet."

I spent the next five minutes filling her in on what I'd learned, then finished up by saying I was confident Braun was running a brothel staffed by prostitutes he'd hooked on drugs, and that I also thought Annette Fouchet was one of them.

Ari picked up her cup. "But you don't know for sure she's there."

"No."

"How are you going to find out?"

"By posing as a client."

She just looked at me.

I grinned. "Brothels generally display their wares in a living room setting and clients can pick out one they like. I'll know her when I see her."

"Then what?"

"Then to a room where we can talk about breaking her out."

"That's all?"

"Yep. That's all."

She took a sip of cocoa then set her cup on the table. "You think Braun is doing this to support his own habit?"

"I'm not sure he does drugs, so there may be more to it. One thing is certain: a brothel in that location would be a good source of income. He has a newer car and, from what I know, a nice apartment, but that doesn't account for all the money he must be taking in."

"Maybe he gambles."

"Maybe ... I just don't know." And I left it at that.

The rest of the weekend was quiet ... comfortable ... loving. We listened to the radio, took a walk Sunday morning after breakfast, and simply enjoyed each other's company. The plan I had to spring Annette was vague, if she was at the brothel, but at least it was a plan. I'd talk it over with Pepper and Murph on Monday.

TWENTY-ONE

Marcia knocked lightly on Annette's door.

"Who is it?"

"Your next-door neighbor."

"Come in."

Annette was sitting on her bed, a copy of the March 25th *Life* magazine beside her. The front cover had a photo of a fellow wearing a homburg hat and smoking a cigarette in a holder. Looked British.

Marcia smiled and nodded toward the magazine as she sat down. "Fancy-looking fellow, there. Is that your knight in shining armor?"

"No, I'm afraid not. It's some ex-ambassador to Berlin named Henderson who's written his memoirs. I was reading an article about the Pope invoking God's aid for peace in Europe." She paused, looking at the magazine. "Do you believe in God, Marcia?"

Marcia drew a pack of cigarettes and small box of matches from her robe pocket, put a cigarette in her mouth, and lit it. "Well ... yes and no."

Annette laughed. "That's a hell of an answer."

"It's an honest one, at any rate. If you mean do I believe in a personal God that grants favors to people who ask for them, or some old fogey with white hair and a long beard who created people on a whim, then the answer is no. I will say the Old Testament God appeals to me somewhat. He was quite human at times. Had a temper and could be a real prick. But generally, most religions don't make much sense to me, even if they make you feel good one day a week. Speaking of feeling good, you sound better. How do you feel?"

"Better than a couple days ago ... A little anxious, but better. Bertha cut back on what she gave me. Didn't say so but I can tell. She said you talked with her about me but that's all she said. No details. I asked but she said to talk with you."

Marcia took a drag on her cigarette and blew smoke toward the ceiling. "I had a heart-to-heart talk with Bertha. I told her I wanted to get you out of here."

Annette, with an astonished look on her face, opened her mouth, closed it, and swallowed hard. "How would you do that?"

"We'll talk about that in a minute. If you were out of here, do you have any place you could go that would be safe? More importantly, do you have anyone who would help you get clean—get off drugs completely?"

Annette thought for a moment. A tear rolled down her right cheek and she brushed it away with her hand. "No ... No one. I can't return to my aunt's house; she wouldn't have me in the condition I'm in. And in any case, that's the first place Braun would come looking." She paused again, leaned forward and stared at the floor. "The only person I could trust is my mother, but I don't know where she stays. I think sometimes she's at the Bowery Street Mission or one of the doss houses nearby, but I'm not sure."

"She clean?"

"She drinks, but I don't know how much. She doesn't do drugs."

"If you had enough junk to keep you for three days, do you think you could find her?"

"Maybe ... I don't know. You could arrange to get me enough for three days?"

Marcia stood, walked to the small table near the bed, put her cigarette out in the ashtray, and returned to her chair. "Yeah, I think I can."

"Would you come with me?"

"No, honey. Can't."

"Why?"

"Several reasons, but most important is someone has to cover for you. For that matter, someone has to cover for Bertha. That would be me. Braun will go bat-shit crazy. I think I can handle him, at least to the point of only getting slapped around a bit. Nothing new in that."

What she didn't say is she'd managed to take a boning knife from the kitchen and hide it in her room. If Braun really got rough, she'd plant it in his gut.

Marcia leaned forward and took Annette's hand. "Here's the plan. It's pretty straightforward, but listen closely. You've had a couple days off, but tomorrow is Monday and you'll have to go back to what you've been doing. Mondays are generally slow, so I've asked Bertha not to use you unless she has to. Tuesday morning at seven o'clock, you go to the kitchen, and Bertha will fix you up, just enough to take any edge off. You need to be thinking clearly. She'll give you a kit to take with you. Go straight to the back door. I'll be there waiting with a coat and scarf for you. Got that?"

"Yes ... but the back door is padlocked."

"I'll take care of that."

Annette took Marcia's hand in both of hers. "Why are you doing this, Marcia?"

Marcia smiled. "Good question. I'm not too damn sure I know, myself. No ... that's a lie. It's really pretty simple. You don't belong here. You're here in this mess because Braun—that low-life bastard—got you hooked and you had no other choice. He was your only source for coke and horse. Oh, you might have gone to a hospital, but on your own, you'd wind up going cold turkey in a loony ward. Chances are you'd come out more shattered than when you went in. That's why, when you leave, you have to find your mother. From what you've said about her, she's been around the block a few times and is tough. You'll need her."

"What will happen to you?"

"Don't worry about me."

"But Braun—"

"David and I go back a ways. I'll handle him one way or another."

"I'll do everything you say, Marcia. I don't know how to thank you."

"Well, we haven't pulled it off yet, but we will. Just get out of here, find your mother, and get clean. That'll be thanks enough."

TWENTY-TWO

Monday morning, I managed to make it into my office just behind the kid who delivered Danish and coffee from the local deli, and just ahead of Pepper. Not that I wanted to—the bed was warm and so was the body lying next to me—but duty calls.

I shed my coat and hat, set a coffee and Danish on Pepper's desk, and took mine into my office. Before sitting at my desk to enjoy my second breakfast of the day, I went to my stash cabinet and took out a pipe, the Sasieni Jake Resnick had talked me into buying. With a name like Sasieni, I still questioned that it was a British pipe, but Jake, and the fact it was stamped *Made In England*, assured me that it was. It was also stamped *Hurlingham*, and was what I would call chubby, with a thick, slightly rounded bowl that had a gnarly finish. I filled it, walked to my desk and set it in the ashtray as I plopped my butt in the chair.

I had just peeled the lid off my coffee when Pepper came in, hung up her coat and hat and walked to the doorway of my office. "I smell coffee."

"Yours is on your desk with a Danish. Cheese Danish, actually, unless it's different than mine. How's Bo?"

"Pissed!"

I almost said, "What? Run out of bubble bath?" Stopped short. Said nothing.

She wasn't smiling. "They cut him back to three days' work a week. According to his foreman, it's only for a couple weeks, but you never know. Seems as though there's been a change in shipping routes or something like that and it's causing a delay."

"Well, with your increase in pay, it should offset any loss in total income."

"It does, and with his hours cut, I'm making more than he does, and I think that bothers him as well, but he didn't say so. If his short hours only last a couple weeks, everything will be fine. If longer, I don't know ... We've been saving up to buy a house. Maybe get married in the fall and buy a house ..."

Her voice tapered off and I wasn't sure what to say. Her tone told me it was something really important to her. Thinking of something light, I said, "Do you think I could be best man? I'd never make it as a bridesmaid."

She chuckled. "No, you wouldn't. God! The image of you in a dress ..."

"Yeah, we'd better scratch that idea. Get your coffee and Danish and come in here. We have some planning to do."

She settled in at the side chair. "All right, boss, what are we planning?"

"I'm going to visit a brothel this afternoon."

The Danish paused halfway to her mouth. "You serious?"

"Yep. And you're going, too. Well, not into the brothel but I want you along. Murphy will be here at three o'clock. He'll be going as well."

"What are we doing, raiding the place?"

"That's for tomorrow morning if Annette Fouchet is in the brothel."

"Better fill me in, boss. I'm lost."

I told her about the four of us, myself, Murph, Jake, and Elle, making the rounds on Saturday trying to identify the brothel run by Bertha, and having no luck. I mentioned that I might have spotted Braun but wasn't sure. Then I told her about Vivian Spaulding, stepping in between her and some thug who wanted to improve her looks by banging her head on my taxi, and her message about the house on Fifty-first between Ninth and Tenth Avenues. An unattached brownstone with a green door.

"We're going to hire a taxi, with a specific taxi driver if I can arrange it. The driver's name is Milly. You'll stay in the taxi out front and I'm going to send Murph around back to check on back doors or other exits while I try to make a connection inside."

"Milly?"

"She was driving the cab when I had that little disagreement with the boyfriend, customer, pimp, or all three, of Vivian Spaulding. Milly is smart, streetwise, and offered her services as a driver. Gave me a phone number where I can get hold of her."

"So ... what are Milly and I supposed to do while you're inside playing house?"

"Keep a lookout for Braun. You know what he looks like. If you spot him coming in, have Milly lay on the horn three times, long, like she's been waiting on a fare. Braun knows me because of that slapping incident in front of the tobacco shop the other day. I don't want him to see me and I don't want a confrontation, but at least I'll know he's coming and maybe I can find a way to slip out unnoticed. If I can't, I'll play it by ear. It could go downhill in a hurry. I have a gut feeling he carries a gun."

"Well, if I hear shots, I'll come in and save your butt."

I smiled. "Not a doubt in my mind, partner, not a doubt in my mind."

The Nude on the Postcard

She picked up her Danish and coffee, headed for her office then stopped in the doorway. "I translated the letter Elle gave us Friday. I'll get it as soon as I finish breakfast."

She was back in a few minutes and laid the original letter in front of me. I set my coffee on the desk and picked it up.

Mon chéri,

Enfermé dans ce petit paquet est un cadeau pour vous, celui que je crains que vous aurez besoin de beaucoup plus que moi même. Vous devez quitter la France, vous devez échapper à la tempête venant de l'est, une tempête qui va sûrement engloutir tous ceux qui restent dans notre pays. Je vous prie, allez à l'Amérique. Nulle part ailleurs sur le continent, ou même l'Angleterre, sera sur. Les gemmes devraient sein assurer votre passage, peut-être pas dans le style, mais à coup sûr en toute sécurité. Nous avons apprécié l'autre au cours de la dernière année. Peut-être, quand cette agitation a pris fin, nous allons à nouveau.

André

I looked at Pepper. "I get the *Mon Chéri* part but that's my limit. What does it say?"

"Well, boss, as I told you Friday, my French hasn't been used for a while and to be honest, it wasn't all that good to begin with, but here's my translation." She handed me a leaf of notebook paper that read:

My Darling,

Enclosed in this small package is a gift for you, one that I'm afraid you will need much more than I. You must leave France, you must escape the coming storm from the east, a storm that will surely engulf all who remain in our country. I beg you, go to America. Nowhere else on the continent, or even England, will be safe. The gems within should assure your passage, perhaps not in style, but assuredly in safety. We have enjoyed each other over the past year. Perhaps, when this turmoil has come to an end, we shall again.

André

I handed it back to her. "So, unless she wrote it herself, it appears legit."

"I'd say so."

"How's our bank account?"

"Good, for now."

"Let's just hold onto the stone, then. If we decide to sell, we'll shop it around a bit. Is it in the safe?"

"I put it in there after I got the appraisal."

"We'll just leave it there for the time being. Right now, I think we're out about eighty bucks in expenses. If we can pull this off on Tuesday, we'll probably owe her some money back."

Pepper returned to her office. I took a sip of coffee then lit my pipe. I was wondering how much I should involve the FBI if what I had planned worked out. I had no idea how much they had on Braun—whether they could arrest and hold him, or if they were simply in the information gathering stage. Might be good to find that out.

But first, I'd better see if I could line up Milly for the afternoon. I picked up the phone and dialed the number she'd given me. After five rings, I was ready to hang up when a man answered. Over a lot of noise in the background, he hollered, "Body shop!" into the phone.

"I'm trying to get hold of a cab driver named Milly. Is she there?"

"Yeah. Think so. Just a minute."

It was more than a minute, but then I heard the phone drag across something and a voice that said, "This is Milly."

"Milly, this is Max Grant. Remember me?"

"How could I forget? That was more excitement than I'd had in a month. What can I do for you, Mr. Grant?"

"I need a taxi and driver for several hours this afternoon about three o'clock. You free?"

"Sure. Where do you want me to pick you up?"

"My office. Do you still have my card?"

"Yeah. Think so. Hold on ... Yeah. On Flatbush, right?"

"That's right. I'll have a couple people with me and we'll be going to Fifty-first Street."

"I'll be there at three."

After hanging up the phone, I picked up my pipe, dumped the ash, refilled it and set it in the ashtray. No sense lighting it now.

I picked up the phone and dialed the FBI office. Got the same guy as last time.

"Federal Bureau of Investigation, Agent Owens speaking."

"Is Tom Sawyer in?"

"Who's calling, please?"

"Max Grant."

"One moment, please."

And again like last time, a click, no other sound, and then, "Sawyer speaking."

"Max Grant. You have time for coffee? I'll buy."

"Sure, as long as you're buying. Thirty minutes?"

"See you then." I hung up, got up, and walked out to Pepper's office.

"Our cab driver, Milly, will be here about three. I'm going to have coffee with Sawyer of the FBI. I'd like to know just what they have on Braun that I may not have been told, and if they're ready to make an arrest. Not that it makes a helluva lot of difference to what we intend to do but it would be good to know if they plan to pick him up in the next day or two."

I took my hat and coat off the rack, put them on, and then went back in my office for my pipe. As an afterthought, I hit the stash cabinet for a pack of cigarettes, remembering that Sawyer asked for one last time we met. Nothing like being friendly when pumping someone for information.

TWENTY-THREE

It took me a few minutes to flag a taxi, and though it wasn't much of a ride to Tom's restaurant, Sawyer was already sitting in the same booth as before. Two coffees were on the table. I slid in without taking off my coat and set the pack of Luckys on the table. "Just in case you forgot your own again."

Sawyer smiled as he tapped a cigarette out of the pack. "I didn't but I'll take a free one. FBI salaries aren't what they should be. What's up?"

I took a sip of coffee and, without preamble, said, "I'm about eighty percent sure I know where Braun lives and more than ninety percent sure I know where his brothel is."

Sawyer lit his cigarette, took a deep drag and blew smoke toward the window. "And you're going to provide me with this lovely information out of the goodness of your heart."

"No."

"All right. What do you want?"

"Two things. Some in-depth information on Braun—more than the vague spy story you gave me last time we met—and a promise."

Sawyer winced and sighed at the same time. It was kinda funny. He tapped the ash from his cigarette into the ashtray. "This is almost one of those if-I-tell-you-I'll-have-to-kill-you situations."

"Well, we wouldn't want that. I know one woman who would be very disappointed, maybe two. You have a pen and paper, or just rely on memory?"

Sawyer reached to an inside pocket, took out a small pad and pen. I set my pipe on the table and took a sip of coffee. "Braun is living in Bay Ridge on Sixty-eighth Street." I gave him the address. "And you were right about his madam. It's Bertha who's running the brothel for him on Fifty-first between Ninth and Tenth Avenues. Hell's Kitchen. It's an unattached brownstone with a green door. Now, I'm almost certain the girl I'm looking for is at the brothel. I'll confirm that today. If she is, I'm going to get her out tomorrow morning. The information I just gave you is solid. I need some assurance the FBI isn't going to raid the place or pick up Braun before tomorrow morning."

Sawyer finished scribbling, put his cigarette out, and leaned back. "No, we're not going to arrest Braun or raid the brothel anytime soon. In fact, we would never raid the brothel. That's a job for the locals. I don't have any idea what we'd do with a truckload of hookers anyway."

I smiled. "I could suggest something, but J. Edgar probably wouldn't approve."

He smiled back. "No, probably not." He lit another cigarette, this time, one of his own. "I'm going to tell you a few things. I don't think they're directly related to your present case of the missing girl, but you might stumble across something we have an interest in, and I wouldn't want you to screw it up. First, though, I want you to understand that if you ever share this information with anyone, and I mean anyone, and we learn of it, you'll never practice your profession in New York, or anywhere else in the country again. Understood?"

I nodded my head.

"Say it." I saw a hardness in his eyes that hadn't been there before.

"I understand."

"Good." He paused and looked over his shoulder. The booths behind and in front of us were empty. Quietly, his voice just above a whisper, he continued. "Braun is a zealous supporter of the German cause, a closet Nazi, if you will. He's not a spy, at least in the normal sense, but he provides a substantial amount of money and information for the cause. We estimate somewhere between three and four thousand a month in addition to the shipping and military information he or his girls manage to pick up. He passes this to a man named Frank Geiger every week at predetermined locations. Geiger has other sources for cash as well and takes a cut of the money, though we don't think it's substantial. He then passes money and information on to a man named Paul who lives on Ninety-second Street in Yorkville, upper Manhattan. That's an area you probably know from your days as a cop as Little Germany or Germantown. From there, the money is dispensed to various agents in and around New York and Jersey, and the information is sent by short wave to Germany or South America."

Sawyer paused again, stubbed out his cigarette and took a sip of coffee. "Sooner or later, we're going to be at war with Germany. Hell, we're almost in it now because the only thing keeping England afloat is the tremendous amount of supplies we send them—not only military, but also food, grain, and cotton for clothes. The problem is the supply convoys are vulnerable in the mid-Atlantic from German U-boats, and thousands of tons of supplies are lost in addition to the gutsy fellows who man the merchant ships."

I relit my pipe, which had gone out while I was listening. "So why don't you arrest these bastards, or deport them, or give them lead poisoning?"

"Lead poisoning?"

"Yeah. Thirty-eight caliber in the ear."

He chuckled. "Never thought of that. I'll pass it on. In reality, this is a case of better the spy you know than the spy you don't know. On occasion, we've been able to feed them false or misleading information—don't ask how—and we can track these guys and monitor their radio communications. As a result, we can change shipping schedules or routes. Well, the FBI can't, but the government office in charge of shipping can. In fact, they just did. They put a ten-day hold on a convoy that was supposed to load and ship this week."

"I heard about that."

Sawyer's head came up. "You did? How? Where?"

Not wanting to get Pepper in any trouble, I thought for a few seconds before saying anything. "Not exactly about a hold on shipping, but my associate's boyfriend works on the docks. His days have been cut. He was told it was because of a shipping change. That's all, but it ties in with what you say."

"That's all right, then. Normal procedure. Hmm ... Just to satisfy my curiosity, tell me how you're going to cut your girl loose from the brothel. I mean, a fella just can't go waltzing into a whorehouse, pick one of the gals up, and dance out."

"With some brothels you could if the price was right, but not this one, I'm sure. This afternoon, after the three o'clock shift change at the base, I'm going to show up at the brothel as a customer and ask for Annette. I'll say she was recommended by a buddy of mine. Once I get her alone, I'll tell her who I am and that her mother has hired me to get her out, and that I'm planning to do that the following morning early. It'll also give me a chance to look around. All those homes have back doors. Whether they keep theirs locked, I don't know, but I'll bet they do—maybe even barred and bolted to keep the girls from wandering off. I don't want to try a breakout during the day, today. For all I know, the madam running the place carries a gun, and there's always a chance Braun may be there, or drop in, and I'll bet he's armed. Early tomorrow morning seems to be the best bet."

Sawyer drank the last of his coffee. As he set his cup down, he asked, "You still have friends on the police force?"

"Yeah, a few. Why?"

"You might be wise to ask if they have any unofficial information on Braun."

"Like what?"

"Like you may be interested that one or more of the women he dated, who later disappeared, washed up on the shore of the Hudson with their throat cut. We're not involved. That's another matter for the locals, but we hear things and occasionally share information."

I thought about that for a moment. "All right, let me ask a serious question. What impact would it have on your operation if Braun were to meet with a serious accident ... a fatal accident?"

"Like lead poisoning?"

I nodded. "Something like that. I'm not saying I'm going to go looking for the guy just to put him on a slab at the morgue, but believe me, if Annette Fouchet is in that brothel today, I'm going to get her out tomorrow no matter what it takes. If Braun is there, and objects, I'll put him down."

Sawyer took another cigarette out of his pack, looked at it then put it back. "I smoke too much ... I'm not sure what impact it would have. Maybe none. We don't believe Braun is directly involved in any espionage. It would certainly have an impact on Frank Geiger's source of funds. He'd probably feel a need to replace him, but I think we'd pick up on a replacement quickly. Obviously, the agency can't appear to sanction something that might look like a Murder Incorporated hit, but personally, I understand you have to do what's necessary to get your girl out as soon as you can. If you don't, she may not be there, and then you'd be searching for the body of a dead daughter, not a live young lady."

I took one last sip of coffee, put fifty cents on the table for the coffee and tip, and put my pipe in my pocket as I stood up. "All right, then. If I find anything tomorrow I think may be of interest to you, I'll call you."

"Call me anyway. Let me know how you made out."

As I headed out the door to hail a cab back to the office, I was thinking it might be a good idea to phone Sergeant Belden and ask about Braun and missing women. It occurred to me Braun might be getting rid of them for any number of reasons, not the least of which might be they weren't bringing in enough money. It also occurred to me that I was hoping the bastard would be there in the morning.

TWENTY-FOUR

Though it was early in the day, David Braun sat in his living room, sipping a very light scotch and water while listening to news on his radio. He wasn't particularly interested in local stuff, but the international news held his attention: The Anglo-French war council had met in London and agreed that neither Britain nor France would make a separate peace with Germany. And that warmonger, Churchill, had given a strong anti-German speech in the House of Commons. It was rumored that Germany was preparing to invade Norway and that other Scandinavian countries would be next.

Braun sipped his drink and smiled. The Fatherland was on the move, and he doubted whether the British or French would be able to stop the tide of Nazism. Frank Geiger told him several times how important his efforts were in providing funds for their American operation, but he wished he could somehow do more. He even dreamed once that he'd gone to Germany and been made a captain in the SS. The dream was so convincing that, on waking, he believed he was in Germany, but was soon disappointed to find he was still in New York. So disappointed, in fact, that Bertha and the whores on Fifty-first Street paid for his foul mood when he visited later in the day.

His thoughts turned to the brothel and the meeting early next morning with Frank. He wondered why Frank wanted to talk with Annette Fouchet. All he'd said was that she'd worked at Columbia University, and Braun had no idea why that might be important. That worthless bitch! He'd been tempted to get rid of her when Bertha told him she'd given Annette a couple days' rest because she'd been sick, and it had been pure luck that he hadn't. Frank would have been pissed. Bertha also told him it had been Marcia who'd brought Annettte's condition to her attention. Another interfering bitch who'd better watch her step. He'd have had a little chat with Marcia but she'd been with a customer and he was in a hurry. I'll talk with her later in the morning tomorrow after we're done with Annette, he thought, but if that bitch shoots her mouth off, it'll be her taking a few days off. Come to think of it, Bertha was acting a little strange. Very closed mouth. No chitchat. All business. Maybe she wanted more money. He'd have to think about that, but didn't see it as a problem. It would be cheaper to pay more than to replace her.

And replacements were another complication. He'd lined up three. Two additional and one to replace Annette, but depending on what Frank wanted to do with her, he might only have room for two. And then a thought occurred to him, one so startling he wondered why he hadn't made a connection before: how did Frank know Annette was one of the women at the brothel, and how did he know she'd been employed by Columbia University?

He sat up straight and placed his glass on the table next to him. It could be one of the whores ... no, too difficult for one of them to get that information out, except maybe by the telephone he had installed. But the timing would have to be perfect because the phone was in the kitchen, and Bertha spent most of her time there except during the busy hours of the evening. Bertha! Had to be Bertha. So Frank the spy had a spy in his brothel. The thought struck him as funny for some reason, and he laughed out loud. Well, he'd have a serious conversation with Bertha, but not until after Frank's business was conducted the next morning. In the meantime, he had a delivery of some coke and horse to make to his newest conquest. Cute little fair-skinned blonde. What was her name again? Ah yes, it was Peach, Wanda Peach. He'd had her laughing when they went out Saturday afternoon, after a morning romp, because he insisted on calling her peaches and cream. And she was certainly that.

TWENTY-FIVE

I ducked into a phone booth just outside the restaurant and called my office. Pepper picked up on the second ring. "Is my associate hungry?"

"Just thinking about transferring calls to the answering service for an hour. Didn't know how long you'd be gone."

"Ruben and Coke sound good?"

"Fine. Probably what I'd order anyway."

"I'll pick up a couple at the deli. If I get them here, they'll be cold by the time I get to the office. See you in about thirty minutes."

When I walked into the office with lunch, Pepper was sitting at her desk cleaning her Browning .32 automatic.

I hung up my coat and hat then nodded toward my office. "Let's eat in there and we can talk over lunch."

"Be there in a minute, as soon as I put this baby back together."

Pepper actually has two automatics, a .32 and a .380, but preferred the .32 even though it's a smaller caliber. She says she's more comfortable with it. There's something to be said for that. I often carry my .38 snubnose as a precaution, but if I know I'm going into a situation where there's some likelihood I'll have to use a gun, I carry my .45 automatic. It's a hell of a lot noisier than the smaller .38 but it always gets the job done, and the comfort level can't be beat.

She came in and sat in the side chair next to my desk as I was popping the caps on the Cokes. I asked where her Browning was.

"Locked in my desk drawer. I thought it might be smart to take it with me this afternoon."

"Won't hurt, but I can't imagine you'll need it. Tomorrow may be different."

"How so?"

"However I manage to get inside in the morning, I want you with me. I don't know what kind of shape Annette will be in and just having you there might make a difference."

"I take it Elle isn't going to know about this."

"Nope."

"She won't like not being told."

"Too bad. I can't take a chance on her screwing things up. I wouldn't mind having Jake along but they're living together and I can't take a chance on him, either. Today should be simple, or at least I hope it will be. Murph should be here in about an hour and Milly soon after. We'll leave about three."

"And I wait out front in the taxi."

"Yeah. It'll give you a chance to get acquainted with Milly. I think you'll like her. You might want to take the picture of Braun with you, the one from the roll I had developed. Show it to Milly. That reminds me, we need to get the camera and copies of the photos back to Annette's aunt. Maybe after tomorrow, we can do that."

I took a sip of Coke. "How's Bo doing?"

"He's all right. They told him that after this week they'll go back to regular hours with probably some overtime." She smiled. "I knew things were looking up Saturday night when he suggested going out to dinner one evening this week. We'll get married and maybe start looking for a house to buy in the fall, just a bungalow in a nice neighborhood."

"Kids?"

"Not for a while. Few years."

I didn't say anything but breathed an inward sigh of relief. I didn't want to lose Pepper. Oh, I knew it might happen eventually, but a few years sounded good to me. We finished our lunch and I decided to call the Sixty-eighth Precinct to see if I could get hold of Sergeant Belden.

"Sixty-eighth Precinct, Adams."

"Jeez, Ron, they ever let you out in the fresh air?"

"Only coming in or going home. This Grant?"

"Yeah. Is Belden in?"

"Yep. He's in the can. You want to hold on?"

"I'll wait."

"Could be two minutes or two hours. Depends on what he's reading."

"I'll wait." I heard a click and then silence. About a minute later, a click and a voice.

It was Belden. "Grant?"

"Yeah. You must not have been reading the *Times*."

"Why's that?"

"Adams said you were in the men's room, reading. Might be two hours."

"I was reading the wanted bulletins. Didn't take long. Whatcha need?"

Since Belden had originally suggested Agent Sawyer, I didn't think there was any need to keep his name out of it. "Tom Sawyer thought it would be a good idea to call you and ask about any connection between David Braun and some missing women."

There was silence for a few seconds. Then: "I checked my notes and I did talk with him once. We suspect he may have been involved in at least two missing persons cases and one murder over the past year. There may have been more, but we were able to trace the movements of all three, and at one time all three had worked as hookers in a brothel we know he owns. We talked to him several months ago but have nothing to tie him to the murder or the missing women. He admitted knowing them, but that was all. Personally, I think he offed all three, and maybe others we don't know about, but without proof, we can't arrest him. He's a cold bastard, I'll tell you that. At the end of the interview, he just smiled, shrugged his shoulders, and said, 'You know how those women are—here today, gone tomorrow.' And then he laughed out loud. It would have been a great pleasure to punch that little twit into next week but I had a detective lieutenant with me so I didn't do anything. You still looking for that missing girl?"

"I may have found her. I'll try to confirm that later today. I think she's in a brothel not far from the docks and naval yards."

"How you going to confirm that, knock on the door and ask?"

I could hear the smile in his voice. "Something like that. I'm going to pose as a customer and request her based on hearsay from a buddy."

"You going to get laid as part of the bargain?"

"Not planning on it."

"I remember from high school a quote about best laid plans or best plans laid—something like that."

I laughed out loud. "All you remember is the 'laid' part, fella."

"Yeah, well, when opportunity knocks ..."

"That's an opportunity I don't need. Thanks for the information."

"Let me know how you make out, will you?"

"I'll call you later in the week."

I hung up, picked up my pipe, lit it, and walked out to Pepper's office to put on a pot of coffee. I could use a cup and figured Murph would be here soon.

She looked up from the account book she was working on. "That a new pipe?"

"Not really. I just don't smoke it often. It's a Kaywoodie."

"Strange shape. All angles."

"It's called a Bulldog. Don't ask me why. I haven't the foggiest idea. While I'm thinking of it, and since you're doing the books, I'm going to take a hundred in cash out of the safe."

She laughed. "Planning a party?" I didn't reply, just smiled.

The door opened, Murph walked in, tipped his hat to Pepper, and nodded toward the coffee pot in my hand. "That's a good idea. Colder than a well digger's ass out there and rain that's going to be snow before late evening."

"Hang your coat and hat up. It'll be a bit before we leave." I walked to the bathroom, filled the percolator from the tap, added the basket and coffee, set it on the burner. "Should be ready in a few minutes. Come into my office."

He parked himself in the side chair and I sat at my desk. I told him Pepper would be with us, that we had a special taxi driver for the afternoon, and what I planned to do. "We'll have Milly drive the length of the block and we'll count the houses from the brothel to the intersection of Fifty-first and Ninth Avenue. That's where we'll get out. I want you to walk down the alley behind the houses. You'll have to count them. When you get to the brothel, I want you to go up and try the back door. I'm pretty sure it will be locked, so don't force it. Just check it and look it over good so you can describe it to me. I'll walk to the front of the brothel and make like a customer. You come back to the taxi and get in back with Pepper. Got it?"

"Yeah, Max. No problem."

I went to the safe, counted out a hundred in small bills, rolled them, and put a rubber band around the wad. Then I went to my stash cabinet.

"I'm going to take a small flask of whiskey with me and before we get out of the taxi, we'll both take a hit from it. It wouldn't be unusual for one of their customers to smell a bit like booze. Hell, they probably expect it. In your case, if you were questioned by anyone, just tell them you got your streets mixed up. If you smell like you've been hitting the bottle, they'd believe you."

We sat around for another forty minutes, drinking coffee and hashing over old times at the department before Murph retired and I got canned. I'd just made a short trip to the bathroom to deposit some of the coffee I'd rented, when there was a tap at the front office door and Milly walked in. I made introductions.

I put my peacoat and hat on, slipped a pipe and tobacco pouch in my pocket, and turned to Milly. "You parked out front?"

"Yep."

"Cops might tow your taxi away."

She grinned. "No they won't. I put a sign on my dash. Says 'Medical Pickup.' Walk with a limp when we go out."

Pepper laughed out loud. "This, I gotta see."

When we went out the front door, I didn't see any cops. Didn't limp. We got in the taxi, me in front, and I told Milly to head for Fifty-first and Ninth Avenue.

TWENTY-SIX

We made one pass down Fifty-first Street, spotted the brownstone, and counted houses till we got to Tenth Avenue and stopped just shy of the corner. Before Murph and I got out, we hit the whiskey flask and I told Milly to drive one block farther, turn around and come back to park a couple houses from the brothel on the other side of the street. When we opened the doors, Pepper moved up front with Milly. Murphy slowly walked up 10th toward the alley and I walked back toward the brownstone thinking that I sure hope its a brothel, or the word awkward isn't going to cover the situation.

It was. I must have looked or smelled the part I was playing because a few seconds after I rang the doorbell, a rather large, rather ugly woman with a wart on the side of her nose opened the door, looked me up and down, and said, "Won't you come in?"

I did. She closed the door and I followed her down the hallway. She was swishing as she went, in a long, loose-fitting gown of washed-out green. We passed one door, and she then turned right through an archway into a parlor. There were three women, two in chairs and one on a couch. All young, fair looking, and only in lacy slips. No bras.

The Nude on the Postcard

My guide turned toward me. "I haven't met you before, Mr. ... ?"

"Max. Just Max. No, I've never been here before but your place was recommended to me by one of the fellows I work with on the docks."

"And who would that be, Max?"

Funny how quickly you think when cornered, isn't it? I made it up on the fly. "Jack, though some guys call him Jock. I think his last name starts with a B—Burt, maybe."

She smiled. "Burkhardt, Jack Burkhardt. Yes, we know him. Would you like a drink, Max?"

I silently praised the gods who watch over liars. "Not now. Maybe later." I looked at the three women. No Annette. "Jack told me about one girl he liked, one with long chestnut hair named Annette."

She walked toward the girl on the couch. "Annette isn't available this evening, but this is Marcia. Her room is next to Annette's and they're close friends. I'm sure she would please you."

Marcia stood and held out her hand toward me. "Hello, Max."

She had a soft "come hither" voice and was certainly pleasant to look at. And she had a way of standing with her pelvis thrust slightly forward that was an invitation if I'd ever seen one. I smiled and took her hand. "Pleased to meet you, Marcia."

Holding my hand, she drew me out of the parlor and down the hallway toward the rear of the house. She stopped, opened the door to her room, and with her hand on my shoulder, gently moved me inside. She pointed to a small coat rack. "You can hang your clothes there or just put them on the chair, whichever you like."

"Uh ... Marcia, could you tell me what this costs?"

"Oh, I thought you might know since you talked with Jack, but it's two to ten bucks, depending on what you want. You pay Bertha on your way out."

"Bertha is that ... that woman in the green frock?"

She chuckled. "Yeah, the ugly one."

She started to pull her slip over her head when I said, "Marcia, what would fifty bucks get me?"

She stopped, her eyes narrowed, and the slip dropped back below her hips. "What do you mean?"

"I mean would fifty bucks get me a few minutes' conversation with Annette Fouchet?"

"You know her? Who are you?"

"A friend of her mother's."

Her knees buckled and she sat down on the bed with a thump then looked at me with a stunned expression on her face. "I told her the other day that I didn't believe in God. I may have to rethink that. You want to get her out of here?"

"Yes."

"When?"

"Tomorrow morning, early."

"I had planned to do the same. Seven o'clock before most of the house wakes up."

I smiled. "I may have to rethink the God thing myself. How were you going to do it?"

"Break the lock on the bar at the back door. The front door has an alarm on it. I've made arrangements to get her three days' worth of light doses of coke and horse. That's all I could do. Figured maybe three days would give her enough time to find her mother."

"I can have her with her mother in less than two hours once she's out of here. But I still need to see her now."

She looked at me for a few more seconds then stood and walked to the door. She opened it a few inches and peered out before turning to me. "Stay here."

The Nude on the Postcard

I walked to the door, opened it a bit more, leaned against the jam, and saw Marcia tap on the door of the next room. She entered and closed the door behind her. After a minute or so, I stepped slightly into the hallway wondering if I should disregard Marcia's caution and go to Annette's room. Before I decided, Annette's door opened and both came out. No doubt about who it was. She looked just like a younger version of her mother—a bit haggard, but the spitting image. I stepped into the hallway just about the time a voice from behind me asked, "What's going on here?" I recognized the voice. It was wart-nose in the green smock.

Marcia, quick and experienced, replied, "Max wants to add to the fun and I asked Annette if she was up to it. She said she was all right."

Just then, the doorbell rang and Bertha turned to go back up front, but paused to look at me. "A threesome, huh? It'll cost you double. Go for broke, Max."

I moved back into Marcia's room, followed by the girls. Marcia closed the door but Annette moved directly in front of me. She swallowed hard and then in a whisper, asked, "Is it true you know my mother?"

"Elle? Yes. I know where she is. She's been looking for you for days and she hired me to help her."

"Who are you?"

"Max Grant. I'm a private investigator and I'm going to get you out of here."

"Now?"

"No, I don't think so." I turned to Marcia. "Does Bertha carry a gun?"

Marcia smirked. "Armed to the teeth. She keeps a revolver in a drawer in the kitchen and carries a small automatic somewhere under that smock she wears, probably in her girdle. I don't know for sure, but knowing how tough that bitch is, I'll bet she knows how to use them and probably has."

I looked back to Annette. "I'm not carrying a gun and I don't want to see anyone get shot, particularly me. I planned to get you out tomorrow morning early if you were here. Marcia tells me she was planning the same thing. We'll combine our efforts."

Marcia lit a cigarette. Took a deep drag. "Bertha knows."

I'm sure surprise registered on my face. "What do you mean?"

"She doesn't know about you, of course, but I needed a three-day kit for Annette and a pry bar to take care of the door. Had to have her help."

"And she gave it? What if she tells Braun?"

"Oh, you know about him, too."

"Yeah, quite a bit. Nasty bastard. How'd you convince her?"

"Let's just say I did. You don't need details. In any case, Bertha will lay it all on me. Braun may knock me around a bit but that's all he'll do. And he may suspect Bertha but he'd have a hard time replacing her, so she's safe enough."

I thought for a minute. Then I looked at Marcia. "Let's plan this thing, then. Can you get the bar off the door by six thirty?"

"Yeah, I think so."

"I need better than think so."

"Then yes, I'll get it off."

"We'll be here about seven and come in through the back door. We'll go straight to Annette's room. Annette, you be ready to go before seven. We should be able to get in and out in three minutes. I think you should come with us, Marcia."

"Who is 'us'? Annette's mother?"

"No. Two of my associates. We'll take Annette to her mother."

Marcia took another drag on her cigarette and then put it out in an ashtray. "I think I'd better stay here. I have my own reasons, but one of them is I couldn't get enough stuff to hold me over for a few days. I'd be coming unglued before noon. I'm edgy now and you can see how Annette is."

I looked. Annette's eyes and nose were running. Not much but noticeable. She saw me looking. "Marcia had Bertha cut down on my dose so I'd be thinking clear in the morning, or at least thinking better than usual, but I have a bad stomach ache, and I'm shaky and jittery."

"You'll be all right. You'll have help in the morning." I looked at Marcia. "Has Braun been here today, or do you think he'll be here tomorrow?"

"He'll be in later tonight to pick up the money from last week and the weekend. Probably ten o'clock or so. He may or may not be in tomorrow."

I moved toward the door. "I'd better be going. How much am I going to owe Bertha?"

Marcia laughed. "A threesome? Just give Bertha fifteen bucks and keep walking toward the door. She won't argue."

I reached in my pocket, pulled out the small roll and peeled off fifty dollars. I handed it to Marcia. "You may need this." She started to say something and I just shook my head. I looked at Annette. "Be ready."

As I walked down the hallway, I separated fifteen from my roll, folded it, and handed it to Bertha, who was standing in the parlor archway.

She smiled. "Enjoy yourself, Max?"

I smiled as well. "I'll be back."

TWENTY-SEVEN

I walked out into a light but very cold rain. Milly's taxi was parked on the opposite side of the street, two houses west, and pointed toward Ninth Avenue. Milly saw me and put the taxi in gear. With my back to the brothel, I made a circular motion with my hand and started walking in the opposite direction. I had a gut feeling I was being watched. Probably wasn't, but I didn't want to be seen being picked up in a taxi, so walking toward the docks would seem natural.

Milly got the message and drove past me toward the intersection. I kept walking and turned right when I got to Tenth Avenue. About a minute later she came along side and picked me up. Pepper was still in front, so I got in back with Murph.

Pepper turned around to me. "Well?"

"We're on for tomorrow morning."

Pepper was smiling. "The question is, were you on this afternoon?"

I fished in my coat pocket for my pipe, struck and put a match to it, and in between puffs, said, "You're not ... going to believe ... what happened ... in there."

"Knowing what kind of house it is, I just might. And knowing how much cash you had on you, I can just imagine."

"Before I get into the details—Milly, are you free tomorrow morning, early?"

"Just name the time, Max. I wouldn't miss this adventure for the world."

"Be at my office at six-thirty. That should put us here just before seven."

On our way back to the office, I related everything that had occurred inside the brothel, including descriptions of Bertha and Marcia, as well as almost verbatim the conversations we had in Marcia's room. I'm pretty good at that. Not that I have a photographic memory, but it's a skill I acquired when I was a cop. When we arrived at my office building, Milly again said she'd be sure to arrive by six or in the morning or earlier. She drove off with a honk of the horn, and we went up to my office. After hanging up our coats, Murph headed for the bathroom, and I asked Pepper if she'd like me to warm up the coffee or make fresh.

"Fresh. Only takes a few minutes."

After I got the pot started, I went to my cabinet, took out a bottle of bourbon, brought it into Pepper's office, and set it next to the hotplate.

She looked at me and raised an eyebrow.

I shrugged. "Just some flavoring for the coffee. Better than sugar and cream."

"To each their own, boss. I'll stick with cream."

I started for my office, had a thought, and asked Pepper for a couple sheets of typing paper, thinking it would be a good idea to sketch out the inside of the brothel, or at least as much of it as I'd seen. I was a decent cop and I'm a pretty damn good investigator, but I'm a lousy artist, so it would be rough. I laid out the first-floor rooms of the house as I remembered them. A few minutes later, Pepper and Murph came into my office, Pepper carrying two coffee cups, and as she set mine on the desk, she said, "Murphy sweetened it up for you."

I took a sip then blinked my eyes. "Jesus, Murph! Must be half and half."

He laughed. "Yeah, about that."

I pointed to the sketch. "Let's take a look at this. It isn't to scale but will give you some idea of the layout of the first floor of the house. No idea what's upstairs, but I'm guessing some additional women's rooms. We'll take it from the back to the front because we'll be coming in the back door. On the left are three rooms before you come to the parlor. The first room is Annette's, the second is Marcia's, and I don't know who has the room next to the parlor. On the right as you come in the door are stairs going up and what appears to be a smaller room, probably a bathroom. Then there are two rooms and a next is the kitchen. There's a door between the kitchen and the front door, maybe a large closet, and then another set of stairs going up.

"We'll have Milly take us into the alley and park in back of the house. The back door should be unlocked and the iron bar should be off the door or loose. All three of us will go in. Murph, you stay at the back door near the stairs. Pepper will come with me to Annette's room. She wasn't in very good shape when I saw her this afternoon, and may be worse tomorrow, so you may have to help her out to the car. I'll try to cover us but I want to give Marcia another chance to come with us. I don't think she will, but I owe it to her to ask. As soon as Pepper is out the door with Annette, we follow. Any questions?"

Murph took a sip of his coffee, looked at the cup, and smiled. "Damn, that's good! Yeah, one question. What if Braun or someone else tries to stop us?"

"I've given that some thought. All three of us will be armed, but I don't want any shooting if there's any way to avoid it. Just showing a gun may take care of that. I don't think we'll see Bertha even if she hears us taking

Annette away. And if one or more of the other women pokes their nose out of their room, well ... like I said, just show your gun. That should be enough. Braun, on the other hand, may be a problem, but I doubt he'll be there that early in the morning. Marcia said he'll be at the house tonight to pick up his money from the previous week and weekend, so I can't imagine any reason for him to pop in at that time in the morning. If he happens to be there, I'll handle it. I had one run-in with him several days ago and scared the hell out of him. Maybe I could do it again. I'll plead guilty to looking for an excuse to shoot the bastard, but I'm not going to create one."

Pepper said, "Hmmm ..." I turned to look at her. She went on. "You know how Bo is when it comes to me being involved in anything dangerous, not that this seems like this is going to be, but I'm going to have to roust out about five in the morning and he'll want to know why."

I thought about that for a few seconds. "Tell him we're involved in a case where we have to stake out a location around the clock, that we suspect a missing woman is at that location but we can't get inside to confirm it. You can add that we've hired extra investigators temporarily to help, but still need to be involved ourselves. Also tell him you'll be with me, that we're watching in pairs. I know you don't like to lie to Bo but what you'll be telling him is partially true ... true enough that you don't have to feel bad about it."

"Yeah, that should work. In any case, he's scheduled to work tomorrow so he'll be leaving soon after I do."

I picked up my pipe and lit it. "All right, then, I think we're set. I'm going to spend the night here. Murph, you can go home or sleep on the couch, whichever you like."

"I'll go home. Gotta feed the dog and take it for a walk, but I'll be here early."

"You're late getting out of here as it is, Pepper, so you may as well leave now. I have a couple phone calls to make and then I'll turn it over to the answering service."

Murphy finished his coffee in one gulp, put on his coat and hat, and was out the door in a minute. Pepper was close behind but stopped at the door and looked back at me. "Don't forget to clean the coffee pot."

"Yes, dear." We both laughed.

I sat at my desk, puffing occasionally on a pipe that was warm in my hand but had gone out, and thinking of the old saying, "What can go wrong, will go wrong." What if Annette collapsed? We'd carry her to the taxi. What if Marcia decided to come with us? We'd get enough junk somewhere to help her hang on till we got her to a hospital—if nothing else, steal it from Bertha. Regardless, we should be in and out and on our way in under five minutes. Unless ... Unless someone challenged us. The likelihood was small. Most, if not all, of the women would be asleep. Marcia seemed confident Bertha would keep to her room even if she heard us come in. To my knowledge, that left only Braun, and the chance of him being there was probably one in a thousand. Well, if he shows, I'll just handle it, that's all. Improvise, as they say—with a fist in his mouth instead of a slap. I smiled at the thought.

I picked up the phone and dialed the number for the FBI.

"Federal Bureau of Investigation, Arlan Smith speaking."

Well, now, someone new. "I don't suppose Tom Sawyer is still in?"

"One minute, please."

And that's what it was, almost a minute. "Sawyer speaking."

"Max Grant. I was right about the brothel." I gave him the address. "From the size of the place, they must be running ten or twelve women. I only saw four, though, plus Bertha, of course. My girl is there. I talked with her and I'm going to get her out early tomorrow morning about seven. I don't expect any trouble. In and out. Should only take five minutes or so."

"So ... did you avail yourself of their services?" I could hear the smile in his voice.

"Nope. Missed opportunity. But Bertha thinks I did. I told her I'd be back."

He laughed. "And you surely will. The address you gave me for Braun is a good one. We staked out the place for a few hours today. He was in and out twice. I appreciate that. It'll allow us to keep tabs on him at any rate. Hell, I may hire you to locate Frank Geiger, Braun's contact. He disappeared late last week."

"Well, let me know and I'll send you a price list for our services."

He laughed again. "Good luck tomorrow."

"Thanks."

I hung up and leaned back as I tamped and lit my pipe. "Better call Ari," I mumbled aloud, "but first ..." I got up, went to Pepper's office and rescued the bottle of bourbon. I poured a couple fingers in my empty cup, took a sip, and then reached for the phone. She answered on the third ring.

"Hello?"

"Hi, sweetheart, it's your favorite carpet cleaner."

She laughed. "My only carpet cleaner."

"As much as I'd love to come over to your place, have a bite to eat and then crawl into bed, I won't be able to. I'm going to stay here tonight. I confirmed the location of Annette Fouchet earlier today and we'll get her early tomorrow morning."

I went on to give her the highlights of my visit to the brothel but didn't go into much detail. When I finished, she said, "And all you did was talk?"

"Yep. Scout's honor."

"Well, I believe you but I doubt any of your pals at the local bar would. They'd either laugh you out or throw you out."

"Don't worry. I'm not about to spread that story around. What's for dinner tomorrow evening?"

"Breakfast."

"I'll be there. Love you."

"Love you too, honey."

I tossed off the rest of the bourbon, walked to the front office, locked the door, and then tackled the coffee pot. After drying the pot, I thought about going to the local deli for a sandwich but didn't much feel like it. The thought of walking a full block to and from in a cold rain didn't appeal to me. So instead, I checked the small refrigerator in my bed-sitting room. I was in luck. There was some Swiss cheese, a half loaf of dark rye bread and some mayo. Two bottles of beer as well. I set the cheese and bread on top of the fridge to warm a bit and then went to the phone to call our answering service and transfer incoming calls.

After I fixed my sandwich and set the beer and plate on the small table next to my one and only chair in the room, I turned on the radio and caught a few minutes of news on WABC: The war in Europe wasn't going well for anyone but Hitler ... American officials were preparing a complete report on German propaganda as it refers to the United States ... Bertrand Russell's appointment as professor of philosophy at City College was revoked ... Al Capone had settled in comfortably at a home in Palm Island Florida after a lengthy stay in hospital while being treated for paresis ... And local weather called for a fifty percent chance of snow in the morning.

Hopefully, the snow would hold off till later in the morning. I didn't see it as a complication, but one never knows. The news was followed by the Amos 'n' Andy program, one of my favorites. I love that show. Those two guys can get into more trouble without trying than I can. The difference being that they seem to get out of trouble quickly. Mine tends to stick around. *Amos 'n' Andy* was followed by *Blondie*. I didn't care to listen so switched to WOR for *The Lone Ranger*. I'm a kid at heart. After the Ranger, there wasn't much else on but music, and I wasn't in the mood, so I turned the radio off.

I had a couple novels on the stand beside the bed: *Appointment With Death* by Agatha Christie, *and The Big Sleep* by Raymond Chandler. I wasn't in the mood for the British gentle art of detecting so chose The Big Sleep. That kept me interested till about ten o'clock when I decided it was time to go to bed. I peeled down to my skivvies, and took a minute to wind up and set the alarm clock for four in the morning. More tired than I thought, I dropped off in a few minutes.

TWENTY-EIGHT

My first thought on waking was that the guy who invented the alarm clock should be castrated. Goddamn, it was loud! I moaned, rolled over, sat up on the edge of the bed, and hit the off button on my Big Ben. The silence was damn near as loud. I usually have two thoughts that require immediate attention on waking: pee and coffee. I took care of them in that order. I finished one cup of coffee, poured another, and then took a quick shower in my small stand-up the building owner was kind enough to install.

I finished my shower, toweled off, and slipped on my robe. Glancing at the alarm clock on the table next to my bed, I realized I had some time to kill and decided to clean my .38 snubnose. Not that I'd fired it recently; I hadn't had time to get to the police gun range the boys in blue were kind enough to still let me use, but over time, any firearm will gather dust and lint that could cause a problem. Granted, revolvers like my snubnose were far less likely to jam than an automatic, but why take a chance?

I took my small cleaning kit from the closet, spread a piece of old newspaper on my table, unloaded the gun, set the bullets on the table and then took the grips off. May as well be thorough. After cleaning, I finished with a light coat of gun oil and spun the cylinder. Smooth as silk. I reloaded and was about to return it to my holster when I heard a noise in the front office. I slipped the snubnose in my robe pocket, and walked through my office to Pepper's. A newspaper that had been sitting on the corner of Pepper's desk had slipped to the floor. I picked it up, set it back on the desk, and returned to my bedroom.

As I removed the gun from my robe pocket, I remembered an incident that had happened to me years ago while I was a member of the local constabulary—an incident involving a gun in a bathrobe pocket.

I had pissed off a small-time hood named Bennie Knight. Bennie was a big-time wannabe who had a protection racket, dealt in booze and maybe drugs, though I never caught him peddling, and ran a string of whores along the edge of Brownsville. He wanted to play with the big boys but never made it.

Bennie had a younger brother named Arthur and that's where the trouble started. It was late February, and I was working the three to eleven shift, filling in for one of the men who was down with flu. The weather was cold. No snow, but the temperature was well below freezing. At about seven o'clock, my beat took me along the edge of Brownsville between Sutter and Pitkin Avenues. I was walking along, thinking of how good a bourbon and coffee would taste when I got home, when my daydream was interrupted by a scream from across the street. Now, it isn't unusual for a pimp to slap one of his hookers around if she's holding out on him or not turning as many tricks as he thinks she should, but this guy was working a girl over with a blackjack, doing a number on her head, arms, and shoulders. I slipped my nightstick loose, slid my hand through the leather thong, and hurried across the street.

I came up behind him and tapped him on the shoulder with my stick just as he raised his arm to swing again.

"I think that's about enough, Bud."

He turned. "Who the goddam hell—" That's when he noticed the uniform. "Whadda ya you want, copper?"

"You're being a bit rough on the lady, aren't you?"

"Lady? Shit! But it ain't none of your goddam business. What? Bennie ain't paid you this week?"

I knew who he was talking about. Didn't make any difference. "Nobody pays me but the city. It may not be much but it isn't Bennie's dough."

"Bennie's my brother. Piss off, copper, or he'll waste your ass."

"Not tonight, he won't."

"You son of a bitch!" He raised his arm to take a swing at me.

I didn't swing, I just straight-armed my stick forward and the weighted end smacked him hard right between the eyes. They crossed, and his knees buckled slightly. That's when I slammed him hard with my stick right over his left ear. He screamed and went down, covering his bloody ear with his hand.

I turned to the woman who was leaning against a lamppost. "Can you walk?"

"Yeah."

"Get out of here." She moved slowly down the street.

I reached down, grabbed the front of his coat and raised him up about a foot off the ground. "My name is Max Grant and this is my patch, not yours. Understand?"

He didn't say anything so I repeated myself. He nodded. That's when I laid my stick hard across the bridge of his nose. Heard it crunch. Heard him scream. Dropped him.

I finished my shift, my second of the day, and headed for home, weary and beat but glad the following day was my day off. At the time, I was living in a second-floor apartment on East Ninety-fourth just off Foster Avenue. Nice place, clean, well kept, and not too noisy. It had been a rough day and all I wanted was bourbon, coffee, bourbon, and a bath, in that order. I had the first bourbon while I fixed the pot and put it on the hotplate.

I had a small backup .38 I kept in the drawer of my bedside table that I had been planning to clean for a week. I took it from the drawer and slipped it in my robe pocket. I'd clean it after my bath.

There was a knock at the door. A loud knock. I opened the door and a fist slammed into my chest shoving me back into my room. I didn't fall but was off balance when Bennie Knight stepped in and shoved me again. I fell, got a kick in the ribs and heard the door slam. I got up. Slowly. Bennie was obviously pissed.

"Why'd you beat the shit out of my brother, copper?"

"He came at me with a kosh. What the hell was I supposed to do, kiss him on the cheek?"

"You sayin' my brother's a fag?"

"If he is, that's his problem, not mine."

Bennie pulled a gun from his coat pocket. A big gun. A .45 automatic. "I don't know whether to kill you or just hurt you a lot, copper."

A .45 would do either in short order. I didn't like the odds. I had my hand around the snubnose in my robe pocket and I simply pushed it up toward Bennie raising the front of my robe. "I could shoot you, Bennie."

He laughed. "The old finger in the pocket gimmick, huh? Go ahead."

I did. Right through my robe. I've seen startled expressions on people but the look on Bennie's face was one of total disbelief. The bullet hit him high in the stomach. As he looked down, the automatic slowly slid from his hand and dropped to the floor just ahead of Bennie. I walked over to him, picked up his gun, and said, "Don't go anywhere. I'll call an ambulance."

I went to my pants on the chair, got a nickel from my pocket, and then went down the hall to the pay phone at the top of the stairs. I got the operator, told her I needed an ambulance and to stay on the line because I needed the police as well. Got through to both in short order. They carted Bennie out and I had to make a statement. Nothing came of it for me. Bennie lived, but I never heard from him again. Come to think of it, I never saw his younger brother again, either.

Enough reminiscing, if that's what it could be called. I got dressed and decided to use the belt holster for my .38 snubnose instead of the under-arm shoulder holster. It was simply a matter of comfort and the belt holster was more comfortable. I walked out to Pepper's office, checked the coffee pot, turned the hotplate on low under it, and then went to my desk for a morning pipe.

At about ten till six, I went downstairs, unlocked the front door of the building, and reminded myself I'd have to lock it again when we left. The building maintenance guy would unlock it as usual at seven.

I was back in the office a few minutes when Murphy came in, followed three minutes later by Pepper. She took off her coat and scarf, tossed them on the couch, and headed straight for the coffee pot. "It's cold out there, boss, and starting to spit snow. Not flakes, more like small pebbles."

"Well, if it's just starting now, we should be all right. Let's have some coffee and then go downstairs. Maybe Milly will be a bit early."

She was, but only by a few minutes. As we got into the taxi, me in front, I turned to Milly. "How are the roads?"

"Still good. Shouldn't be any problem getting there on time. Coming back may be different."

"We'll come back to my office but I want you to stay with us till I make a phone call to Annette's mother. I don't know if we'll take her to her mother or if her mother will come to the office. In either case, we may need you."

Milly smiled as she pulled away from the curb. "Ya got me all day if ya need me."

TWENTY-NINE

David Braun arrived at his brothel shortly after six o'clock on a cold, bitter Tuesday morning, keyed the front door's first lock to shut off the alarm, and the second to open the door. The house was silent. He was tempted to go to the kitchen to make a pot of coffee but wanted to be at the front door when Frank arrived. This whole situation with Annette was a mystery, but he assumed everything would be made clear once Frank talked with her.

He was leaning against the front door frame when a cab pulled up. Frank got out, paid the driver, and walked up to the front door as Braun opened it.

"Good morning, Frank."

Frank Geiger nodded and stood to one side as Braun closed the door. "Where is Fouchet?"

"In her room, probably still asleep. I didn't wake her."

"Good. Very good. Is there someplace I can talk with her without perhaps disturbing the other women?"

Braun thought for several seconds. "Yes. Upstairs. The two rooms at the back end of the hall are vacant. We can take her there."

They walked down the hallway and stopped at Annette's door. Braun quietly opened the door and was surprised to see her sitting on her bed, fully dressed.

Her eyes widened, mouth opened, and terror showed on her face. In a voice that was too loud, she said, "What—what are you doing here?" Then she saw Frank. "Who is he?"

Frank stepped forward. "My name is Frank and I would talk with you for a few moments, but not here. Would you come with us, please?"

"Where?"

Braun moved to her and took her arm, pulling her upright. "Upstairs where it's quiet. We don't want to wake the other girls, do we?"

"I don't want to go!"

Braun shook her violently. "You'll go quietly, Annette, or I'll shut you up and drag you."

They walked down the hallway toward the back stairs, Braun half dragging a still reluctant, but now quiet, Annette. Once upstairs, Braun opened the door to the end room, pushed Annette inside, and pointed to a chair beside the bed. "Sit!"

Frank took off his coat and hat, laid them carefully on the bed, and moved in front of Annette. "Now, my dear, I have some questions to ask you ..."

Downstairs, Marcia had heard everything. She stood at her closed door, unbelieving. Braun? At this hour in the morning? And who was that man with him? She heard them talking with Annette. That poor girl must be terrified, she thought. As the three of them came out of Annette's room and moved down the hallway, she opened her door a crack and saw them go upstairs. She was certain Braun would see the bar and lock were missing from the back door—she had removed them shortly after five o'clock—but he had his hands full with Annette and missed it. She didn't dare go upstairs. All she could do now was wait to see if Max Grant arrived at seven or before. Then what?

Annette was staring at the floor. Frank reached out, placed his hand under her chin and raised her head before saying, "*Reacteur a eau lourde*. Does that mean anything to you?"

"It is French."

"And what does it mean?"

"Heavy water reactor."

"Have you seen or heard that term used anywhere? Letters or conversation perhaps, while you were working as a translator at Columbia University?"

Annette said nothing. But Frank, holding her jaw tightly, moved her head from side to side. "Come, come, let us not be stubborn. It will not go well for you. Does the name Joliot-Curie mean anything to you? Letters from him to Dr. Fermi or Dr. Dunning, perhaps? I need to know what was in those letters and you're going to tell me."

Annette remained silent. Frank turned to Braun. "I know this may mean nothing to you, but the French scientist, Joliot-Curie, achieved an atomic fission reaction in January of this year, an indication that a chain reaction might be possible. Our scientists are very interested and are conducting their own experiments. But to continue, we need heavy water. The uranium we have, but the French have obtained all the heavy water available from the Norsk-Hydro Plant in Norway. We believe they are sharing the results of their experiments with the Americans. We want to know if the Americans are going to begin producing heavy water."

He turned back to her, sighed, and without seeming to move, slapped her twice. It took her breath. She opened her mouth but couldn't breathe, and then gagged before falling sideways onto the floor. He looked at Braun. "Pick her up."

Milly parked her taxi directly in front of the three steps leading up to the back door of the brothel and we got out. I went up the steps and tried the door. Marcia had done her job. It was open. I went in, followed by Pepper and Murph, but just as I started to turn to quietly close the door, I caught a movement out of the corner of my eye. It was Marcia, finger to her lips and frantically motioning me to come to her. I pointed to the small alcove opposite the stairs, silently mouthed "wait" to Pepper and Murph, closed the door, and moved down the hallway to Marcia. When I got to her room, she grabbed my arm, pulled me inside, and closed her door.

"Braun is here with another man I've never seen before. They took Annette upstairs."

"Damn! We don't need this!"

"What are you going to do?"

I thought for a few seconds. "We came here to get Annette and that's what we'll do. You pack a bag. Don't argue. If this goes downhill like I think it might, it won't be safe for you here. Stay in your room till I come to get you."

As I walked down the hallway to the alcove, I took my snubnose out. Comfortable as I was with it, I now wished I'd brought my .45 automatic instead. When I got to Pepper and Murph, I whispered, "Braun is here with another man and they've taken Annette upstairs. Pepper, you come with me. Murph, you stay here in the alcove and cover the stairway."

We were halfway up the stairs when I heard a voice say, "Hold her up," followed by several smacks or slaps. At the top of the stairs, we stopped to listen. The voices were coming from the first room on our right.

"I'm getting tired of hitting you, young woman, and you, you're getting tired of being hit, are you not?" Smack! "Now tell me—hold her up, David!—tell me what was in those letters you translated."

I heard a sob, and a very weak, "Let me go ... please." It was like a child's cry. That was all I needed. The door was cracked about two inches and I hit it hard with the flat of my left hand. It flew wide in an arc, banging against the wall, and I stepped into the opening. Braun was standing, holding Annette upright, and another man was standing in front of her, arm raised, ready to swing.

I leveled my snubnose. "Hello, David."

Braun blinked twice like he couldn't believe his eyes. Then his face contorted and I couldn't tell if he was going to cry, or if it was rage. It was rage. He shoved Annette to the side and she collapsed on the floor.

He screamed. "You! You son of a bitch!" And that's when he reached inside his coat.

I yelled, "Don't!" He did anyway.

It was a small automatic and he just cleared his belt with it when I shot him. The slug hit him right center chest and he took one step backward, paused, and then one step forward, still trying to level the gun. I shot again, this time hitting him just left of the first one. He collapsed on the floor, slowly rolled onto his back, his legs in spasms as if he were trying to kick someone, the front of his pants showing a spreading wet stain.

I turned to the other man thinking he might be armed as well, but had no need to worry. He was standing in the same spot, but now with both arms in the air. Pepper was standing just inside the door to my right, her Browning pointed at his middle.

"Should I shoot him, boss?

"Let's get his name for the obituary first. What's your name, tough guy?"

Pepper moved around behind me to Annette, helped her to her feet, and then set her on the bed. She was bleeding from her mouth and nose and had a large welt on her left cheek. The guy in front of me opened his mouth, closed it, then opened it again but all that came out was a croak. He looked terrified with sweat on his forehead that rolled to his eyebrows and down his cheeks.

I tried again. "You got a name, hard ass?"

"Geiger. Frank Geiger."

I remembered his name from my conversation agent Sawyer. Sawyer attached some importance to him but said they'd lost track of him somehow. But here he was, beating up on a young woman in a brothel. I transferred my snubnose to my left hand and took a step closer to Geiger. "I don't know why you're here. I don't care why you're here. But I do care that you've beaten the hell out of that young woman." That's when I hit him. Nice straight right to the nose. I didn't hear it crunch, but the blood started flowing immediately. He started to reach for his hip pocket and I raised my gun.

He stammered, "My, my, my handkerchief."

"Go ahead."

He pulled it out and held it against his nose. Blood was dripping from under his hand to the front of his shirt and he glared at me over the handkerchief. I couldn't help thinking, this is one mean, evil bastard, but I'd made up my mind.

"Listen up, Frank. I'd like nothing better than to put a bullet in you and leave you for the guys from the morgue to clean up, but I'm not going to do that. Get your coat and hat and get out of here."

He did. Didn't even bother to put them on and was gone in ten seconds. I turned to Pepper and Annette. "I'll help you get her downstairs and into the taxi."

We were just shy of the top of the stairs when I heard Murph shout, "Hey!" followed by a shot, and the sound of a falling body.

"Murph? You all right?"

"Yeah. Some guy came down the stairs, pulled a gun from his coat pocket, turned and pointed it up to where you are. Didn't see me in the alcove. I hollered. He spun around toward me and I shot him. I think he's dead ... Yeah, he's dead."

When we got to the foot of the stairs, Geiger's body was lying in a heap. We stepped over him and I turned to Murph. "You help Pepper get Annette to the taxi. I'm going to get Marcia and then make a phone call if there's a phone in the house."

I tapped on Marcia's door. "It's Max."

She opened it and stood there, coat on and bag in hand. "I heard shooting. What happened?"

"Later. Is there a phone in the house?"

"In the kitchen."

"Where's Bertha's room?"

"Next to the kitchen."

When we got to Bertha's room, I banged on the door. "Bertha! Open up!"

She did, and she was still wearing the green smock. She looked at me and said, "I thought there was something fishy about you."

I didn't mince words. "Braun is dead upstairs and there's a body in this hallway. We're going to the kitchen and you're going to put together a week's worth of junk for Marcia. I'm going to call the cops. Go!"

After we got to the kitchen, I gave Bertha a couple minutes to put a kit together for Marcia, then picked up the phone and dialed the operator. "Get me the police. This is an emergency." I gave the address to the officer who answered and told him a couple men had been shot. Then I hung up and turned to Bertha. "You're out of a job. Might be smart to get out of here."

We left Bertha in the kitchen staring after us as we walked quickly down the hallway and out the door and got into Milly's cab. It was crowded, but no one seemed to care. I told her to drive to my building.

Milly dropped us off and then went to find a place to park the taxi till we needed it again. Between Pepper and myself, we managed to get Annette up three flights of stairs to my office, and Marcia joined the two of them as they went into the bathroom. Pepper would help clean her up, but I think she also needed a fix. Marcia would see to that.

I asked Murph to put a pot of coffee on. I went to my stash cabinet, relieved it of a bottle of bourbon that I set on the table with the pot along with some glasses and cups. Then I went to my desk, picked up the half-full pipe that was in the ashtray, lit it, sat back, and closed my eyes. I've been shot, shot at, and shot several men. None of it was good when it happened. Worse when it was over. I've never had any regrets, particularly over scum like Braun, but taking a life, any life, leaves you with doubts ... for a while, anyway.

I picked up the phone and dialed the number of Elle's boarding house. I didn't count, but it must have rung ten times. It was Elle who finally answered.

"Elle?"

"Grant? You asshole! Why didn't you call me yesterday like you promised?"

"I couldn't."

"Why not?"

"Because if I had, I wouldn't have lied to you. We knew where Annette was yesterday afternoon and you would have wanted to get her out then. That would have screwed things up, maybe got her or yourself killed. As it was, it wasn't nice, but she's here now with us in my office."

"Oh, God! Oh, God, Jesus! Can I talk with her?"

"She's in the bathroom with Pepper getting cleaned up. Listen, Elle, she's not in good shape. She was physically beaten and she's hooked on drugs, most likely horse and coke. She's going to need a firm but gentle mother, a friend, probably for a long time. I think you can be that person, but I wanted you to be aware of it before you see her. Is Jake with you?"

"Yes. He's standing next to me."

"All right then, get a taxi and come to my office."

"As quick as we can." She hung up.

I stood, relit my pipe, and walked out to Pepper's office. Murph was sipping from a cup. He smiled, said, "No, the coffee isn't ready yet, but the bourbon is."

I smiled back. "I'll wait." I looked at the wrinkled face of the retired cop for a few seconds. "I think you may have saved my life today, old friend. Maybe even Pepper's and Annette's. I didn't figure that guy for a gun, or at least I thought he was too damned scared to do anything but get out in a hurry. His name was Geiger, by the way."

Murph set his cup down. "Oh, I think he was scared, and he sure was in a hurry. He half tumbled down the stairs. I'd heard the shots upstairs and could hear your voice so I knew you must be all right. When the guy—Geiger, you say?—got to the bottom of the stairs, he stopped, put on his hat and coat and made like he was going to go down the hallway to the front door. I wouldn't have stopped him if he had, and in any case, he hadn't seen me. But he took a couple steps, stopped, and went back to the stairs. He took an automatic out of his coat pocket, leaned against the wall, and aimed the gun up the stairs. I knew you'd be coming down. I stepped out of the alcove, raised my revolver, and shouted at him. He whipped around, gun pointed toward me, so I shot him. Didn't see as I had a choice."

I put my hand on his shoulder. "You didn't, Murph. You surely didn't. Thank you."

"When we were coming back in the taxi, you said you called the cops. Give 'em any names or identify yourself?"

"No ... but there are a couple fellows who will figure it out pretty quick. One of them is FBI and the other is Sergeant Belden. I don't think either of them will follow it up, though, at least not officially."

Pepper, Marcia, and Annette came out of the bathroom at the same time Milly walked in the front door. I waved and then turned back toward the bathroom. Annette looked better. No blood anyway, but the left side of her face was bruised and a pale shade of red and purple. Pepper was holding her by the hand and brought her over to me.

She let go of Pepper's hand and took mine. "I want to thank you, Mr. Grant. I thought David and that other man were going to kill me. That other man kept asking about translations of letters from French scientists, but I didn't tell him anything. It wasn't because I didn't want to tell him, it was because I couldn't remember." She paused. "They would have killed me, wouldn't they?"

"Braun probably would have. He was suspected of having murdered at least three of the women who worked in the brothel. The other man's name was Geiger, Frank Geiger. He wasn't any better than Braun and in some ways, maybe worse. But that's all over now. Your mother is on her way here and should arrive in a few minutes. The coffee's ready. Would you like a cup?"

"I'd love it. Just black."

Pepper chimed in. "Go sit on the couch. I'll bring it to you." As Annette walked to the couch, Pepper turned to me. "Marcia fixed her up while we were in the bathroom. Gave her a shot. She'll probably be good till late this afternoon or evening. Do you think her mother will be able to handle it?"

"Yeah, I think so. Elle's tough. Been through a lot herself, so I don't think she'll judge Annette. And I think they trust each other. If not, they can learn." As Pepper poured coffee, I looked around. "Where's Marcia?"

"I think she went into your office when we came out of the bathroom. Said she wasn't feeling well. Didn't look too good, either."

I went back into my office. Marcia was sitting in a side chair next to my desk, slightly bent over. I put my hand on her shoulder. "You all right, Marcia?"

She raised her head, smiled, and said, "No." She was quiet for a moment. Then she went on. "I didn't have my usual dose this morning, and after we got here, I thought maybe I could hold out for a while, get started on withdrawal, but I'm feeling a bit ragged already."

I went around the desk to my chair, sat, and put my pipe in the ashtray. "I don't have any firsthand experience in such things but after everything that's gone on yesterday and today, I sure as hell don't think its a good idea to add to the emotional seesaw. How much stuff did Bertha pack for you?"

She picked up her bag and checked without taking anything out. "A week's worth, maybe ten days if I stretch it out ... taper off. I really want to quit."

"Do you have any place to go? Any place safe?"

"No. But I do have that fifty you gave me yesterday. I can find a place."

"Maybe I can help. I have an idea. In the meantime, why don't you pay a short visit to the bathroom and take care of yourself. You'll feel better, and the coffee is fresh."

About two minutes later, the front door flew open and Elle rushed into Pepper's office. She looked around and froze like a statue when she saw Annette getting up from the couch. What followed was several shouts of "Mama, Mama," and at least one "Oh, my baby." I hid out in my office. Jake noticed me, waved, and I motioned to him to come in. We shook hands and I pointed to the chair Marcia had just vacated.

"Quite a family reunion out there."

Jake smiled. "Elle was a lot more worried than she let on. But several times late last evening, she said something was going to happen. Women's intuition, maybe. I gotta tell you, though, she sure was pissed when you didn't call. I told her you were probably busy trying to confirm where Annette was but she didn't simmer down much. After she got off the phone with you today, she told me you knew where Annette was yesterday afternoon."

"Yeah, I did. But I had a plan to get her out and wanted to stick to it. As it was, we ran into a few complications, but it ended well." I paused for a moment. "Tell me, how much room do you have at your apartment?"

"It's one bedroom, bath, kitchen and living-dining area. Not very big, but there's an in-a-door-bed in the living room. You know, the kind that fold down from a closet-like place in the wall. We thought Annette could sleep there. Why?"

"There's a woman we brought with us along with Annette. Her name is Marcia and she's a close friend of Annette's. She's also hooked like Annette but wants to get off drugs. I was thinking if they could stay near each other, or even together, they could help each other out."

"I think the apartment next to us is vacant. Not sure but we can find out. I don't think there's been anyone there since Elle moved in, but if she needs a place, she can move in with us for a few days. We'll make do."

Just then, Elle came in alone. "Make do what?"

Jake turned. "Max was just telling me about a woman named Marcia, a close friend of Annette's, who came out with them this morning. She needs a place to stay for a few days. I told him I thought we could find room."

Elle thought for a couple seconds. "The two of them are sitting on the couch talking. We'll figure out something. I'll tell her to come along with us." She walked around the desk, bent down, and kissed me on the cheek. "You're a crusty old bastard, ya know that?"

I laughed. "That's the nicest thing anyone has said to me all day. Would you like a drink? I have another bottle in the cabinet."

"Nope. I'll pass, and mark this day down. It's the first time I've turned down a drink in years." She paused again. "Annette told me you saved her life this morning. I owe you."

"I'll send you a bill. Actually, I think you have some money coming back. We'll know for sure when we sell the ruby, but it should more than cover expenses."

Jake got up, put his arm around Elle and the two of them walked out to Pepper's office. I just sat back, relaxed, and listened to the low murmur of conversation coming through the door. Eventually, everyone but Pepper and Murphy drifted out.

Murph came into my office. We shook hands. "Helluva day, Max."

"It was that. You going home?"

"Yeah. Pepper gave me fifty bucks. I told her it was too much, but she said she was vice-boss—whatever the hell that is—of this organization and to take it."

I grinned. "She's right. And you deserve it. Stop in later in the week for coffee if you get a chance."

I picked up the phone and dialed the number for the FBI. Sawyer was in. All I said was, "This is an anonymous information call. David Braun and Frank Geiger were killed in a shootout today in Hell's Kitchen."

He replied, "Coffee tomorrow? Ten o'clock?"

"Ten o'clock." I hung up.

A few minutes later, Pepper came in with a cup of coffee and set it on my desk. "I paid Murphy. Paid Milly, too. Gave her thirty bucks. Both said it was too much."

"Ah, well, it's only money."

"You all right, boss? You sound tired."

"I guess I am, but I'll have a quiet evening. Breakfast at Ari's."

"In bed?"

"After. Why don't you go home? I'll turn the phone over to the answering service. We've done enough for the day. I'll wait around here for a while, maybe go to the newsstand on the corner, pick up a copy of the *New York Times* and read it from front to back ... well, look at it anyway."

She was back a minute later in coat and scarf. "See you tomorrow, Max."

"What time does Bo get off?"

"Today? About an hour after I get home." She smiled. "Plenty of time to fix dinner for him and a hot toddy when he hits the front door."

Regis McCafferty

EPILOGUE

After everyone had gone, I sweetened my coffee with a touch of bourbon, sat at my desk with an unlit pipe in my mouth, and stared at the far wall thinking about Sergeant Belden's comment about the best laid plans ... Some wise soul once said, "It's all right to plan plans, just don't plan results." And that short phrase just about summed up our morning. The only things that went well were the taxi ride to the brothel and the back door being open. From there, it went downhill in one helluva hurry. Could it have turned out differently with more planning? No. I was convinced of that. More planning would have meant more time, and it became pretty obvious afterward that time was something Annette didn't have.

Thinking of Belden, I picked up my address book, checked the number of the Sixty-eighth Precinct, and dialed. It was picked up on the first ring.

"Sixty-eighth Precinct, Adams."

"This is Grant, Ron. Is Sergeant Belden in?"

"You two sure are getting chummy."

"Yeah, sometimes friends do."

"I wouldn't know."

"I'm sure you wouldn't, Ron." I didn't like the asshole and he knew it. "Is he in?"

"Hold on."

There was a click, and a few seconds later, another click.

"Belden here."

"Grant." I just waited.

"I think you had a busy morning, Mr. Grant."

"You might say that."

"We got an anonymous phone call early this morning that there had been a shooting at a brothel in Hell's Kitchen. Turns out there were two dead guys, and a madam who didn't know shit. We arrested her as an accessory anyway, but that won't hold up. She'll probably be out of jail by this evening. All she told us was she heard shots, then some guy came into the kitchen where she was, used the phone, and left. Her description of the guy was so vague it could have been anyone. One of the dead guys was David Braun, who we think owned the brothel. We haven't a clue as to who the other one is."

"Frank Geiger."

"Spell it."

"The 'Frank' or the 'Geiger'?"

"You aren't getting any funnier in your old age, Grant."

I spelled Geiger for him. "You in the mood for coffee or bourbon tomorrow afternoon?"

"Both. What time?"

"About four o'clock."

"I'll be there. You take it easy, Grant."

"Yeah—you too."

I hung up, went to Pepper's office, cleaned and dried the coffee pot, and then did what I told Pepper I might do. I slipped on my coat and hat, and went to the newsstand on the corner, picked up a copy of the *New York Times*, and came back to the office.

I sat at my desk, lit my pipe, and looked at the front page. The war in Europe was going well or badly, depending on which side you were on. Hitler was getting ready to pounce on the Balkans; the British wanted to enforce a blockade of the Scandinavian countries; and France was in turmoil as usual. On the local front, La Guardia was proposing a budget of six million less than the previous year, and the Transport Workers Union had deferred a vote for a strike because they were waiting on John L. Lewis to arrive in the city to take over negotiations. It just seemed as though there was confusion and mayhem on all fronts, both home and abroad. I didn't get beyond the front page. I picked up the newspaper, walked to Pepper's office, and laid it on her desk. She'd enjoy reading it in the morning with her coffee and Danish.

I walked back to my desk, took a sip of my drink, and debated taking a shower before going to Ari's for dinner. The dinner she promised would be breakfast. I was looking forward to it. Breakfast usually meant eggs, home fries, and bacon or ham. Always good.

The relationship with Ari was good as well. Serious. Maybe it was time to get more serious. We had tiptoed around the subject of marriage because we seemed to be comfortable with what we had, and marriage would bring changes, some of them major. For one thing, it would probably mean a new apartment for both of us, and yet, we were content with what we had.

The subject was worthy of discussion, but not tonight. Tonight, because Ari was interested, I'd tell her about the happenings of the day, but not in gory detail. She didn't need that and neither did I. And then later ... Later we'd make love. I decided against taking a shower before leaving for Ari's because I remembered she'd bought me some sandalwood bath soap. It would be a perfect ending to an imperfect day.

END

About the Author

Regis McCafferty, freelance writer and author of numerous articles, short stories, and novels, now resides in northern Ohio after having lived in New Mexico for ten years. His previous novel of pre-WWII New York, *The Nude on the Cigarette Case*, was named a Mystery Finalist for the 2015 Indie Book Awards.

THE NUDE ON THE POSTCARD
is also available as an e-book
for Kindle, Amazon Fire, iPad, Nook and
Android e-readers. Visit
creatorspublishing.com to learn more.

o o o

CREATORS PUBLISHING

We find compelling storytellers and
help them craft their narrative,
distributing their novels and collections
worldwide.

o o o

www.ingramcontent.com/pod-product-compliance
Lightning Source LLC
Chambersburg PA
CBHW051248250626
47155CB00009B/3208